UNDERSTANDING DRUGS

Sleep Drugs

TITLES IN THE *UNDERSTANDING DRUGS* SERIES

UNDERSTANDING DRUGS

Sleep Drugs

MALI REBECCA SCHANTZ-FELD

CONSULTING EDITOR

DAVID J. TRIGGLE

University Professor

School of Pharmacy and Pharmaceutical Sciences

State University of New York at Buffalo

CHELSEA HOUSE
An Infobase Learning Company

Sleep Drugs

Copyright © 2011 by Infobase Learning

Chelsea House
An imprint of Infobase Learning
132 West 31st Street
New York NY 10001

Library of Congress Cataloging-in-Publication Data

Schantz-Feld, Mali Rebecca.
   Sleep drugs / Mali Rebecca Schantz-Feld ; consulting editor, David J. Triggle.
     p. cm. — (Understanding drugs)
   Includes bibliographical references and index.
   ISBN-13: 978-1-60413-551-0 (hardcover : alk. paper)
   ISBN-10: 1-60413-551-4 (hardcover : alk. paper)   1. Hypnotics—Popular
works.   2. Sleep disorders—Popular works.   I. Triggle, David J.   II. Title.   III. Series.
   RM325.S33 2011
   615'.782—dc22
                                            2011002972

Text design by Kerry Casey
Cover design by Alicia Post
Composition by Newgen North America
Cover printed by Yurchak Printing, Landisville, Pa.
Book printed and bound by Yurchak Printing, Landisville, Pa.
Date printed: June 2011
Printed in the United States of America

10 9 8 7 6 5 4 3 2 1

This book is printed on acid-free paper.

To the family of my dreams with whom I love to spend my waking hours; to my younger friends who teach me so much about the world I try to shelter them from; to my friends and colleagues for cheering me on, I dedicate this book and this song: "Through all kinds of weather, what if the sky should fall? Just as long as we're together, it doesn't matter at all."

Contents

foreword

THE USE AND ABUSE OF DRUGS

For thousands of years, humans have used a variety of sources with which to cure their ills, cast out devils, promote their well-being, relieve their misery, and control their fertility. Until the beginning of the twentieth century, the agents used were all of natural origin, including many derived from plants as well as elements such as antimony, sulfur, mercury, and arsenic. The sixteenth-century alchemist and physician Paracelsus used mercury and arsenic in his treatment of syphilis, worms, and other diseases that were common at that time; his cure rates, however, remain unknown. Many drugs used today have their origins in natural products. Antimony derivatives, for example, are used in the treatment of the nasty tropical disease leishmaniasis. These plant-derived products represent molecules that have been "forged in the crucible of evolution" and continue to supply the scientist with molecular scaffolds for new drug development.

Our story of modern drug discovery may be considered to start with the German physician and scientist Paul Ehrlich, often called the father of chemotherapy. Born in 1854, Ehrlich became interested in the ways in which synthetic dyes, then becoming a major product of the German fine chemical industry, could selectively stain certain tissues and components of cells. He reasoned that such dyes might form the basis for drugs that could interact selectively with diseased or foreign cells and organisms. One of Ehrlich's early successes was development of the arsenical "606"—patented under the name *Salvarsan*—as a treatment for syphilis. Ehrlich's goal was to create a "magic bullet," a drug that would target only the diseased cell or the invading disease-causing organism and have no effect on healthy cells and tissues. In this he was not successful, but his great research did lay the groundwork for the successes of the twentieth century, including the discovery of the sulfonamides and the antibiotic penicillin. The latter agent saved countless lives during

World War II. Ehrlich, like many scientists, was an optimist. On the eve of World War I, he wrote, "Now that the liability to, and danger of, disease are to a large extent circumscribed—the efforts of chemotherapeutics are directed as far as possible to fill up the gaps left in this ring." As we shall see in the pages of this volume, it is neither the first nor the last time that science has proclaimed its victory over nature, only to have to see this optimism dashed in the light of some freshly emerging infection.

From these advances, however, has come the vast array of drugs that are available to the modern physician. We are increasingly close to Ehrlich's magic bullet: Drugs can now target very specific molecular defects in a number of cancers, and doctors today have the ability to investigate the human genome to more effectively match the drug and the patient. In the next one to two decades, it is almost certain that the cost of "reading" an individual genome will be sufficiently cheap that, at least in the developed world, such personalized medicines will become the norm. The development of such drugs, however, is extremely costly and raises significant social issues, including equity in the delivery of medical treatment.

The twenty-first century will continue to produce major advances in medicines and medicine delivery. Nature is, however, a resilient foe. Diseases and organisms develop resistance to existing drugs, and new drugs must constantly be developed. (This is particularly true for anti-infective and anticancer agents.) Additionally, new and more lethal forms of existing infectious diseases can develop rapidly. With the ease of global travel, these can spread from Timbuktu to Toledo in less than 24 hours and become pandemics. Hence the current concerns with avian flu. Also, diseases that have previously been dormant or geographically circumscribed may suddenly break out worldwide. (Imagine, for example, a worldwide pandemic of Ebola disease, with public health agencies totally overwhelmed.) Finally, there are serious concerns regarding the possibility of man-made epidemics occurring through the deliberate or accidental spread of disease agents—including manufactured agents, such as smallpox with enhanced lethality. It is therefore imperative that the search for new medicines continue.

All of us at some time in our life will take a medicine, even if it is only aspirin for a headache or to reduce cosmetic defects. For some individuals, drug use will be constant throughout life. As we age, we will likely be exposed to a variety of medications—from childhood vaccines to drugs to relieve pain caused by a terminal disease. It is not easy to get accurate and understandable information about the drugs that we consume to treat diseases and disorders. There are, of course, highly specialized volumes aimed at medical or scientific professionals. These, however, demand a sophisticated knowledge base and experience to be comprehended. Advertising on television is widely available but provides only fleeting information, usually about only a single drug and designed to market rather than inform. The intent of this series of books, **Understanding Drugs**, is to provide the lay reader with intelligent, readable, and accurate descriptions of drugs, why and how they are used, their limitations, their side effects, and their future. The series will discuss both *"treatment drugs"*—typically, but not exclusively, prescription drugs, that have well-established criteria of both efficacy and safety—and *"drugs of abuse"* that have pronounced pharmacological and physiological effects but that are considered, for a variety of reasons, not to be considered for therapeutic purposes. It is our hope that these books will provide readers with sufficient information to satisfy their immediate needs and to serve as an adequate base for further investigation and for asking intelligent questions of health care providers.

—David J. Triggle, Ph.D.
University Professor
School of Pharmacy and Pharmaceutical Sciences
State University of New York at Buffalo

1

Sleep: An Introduction

When the ambulance arrived at the hospital after the accident, 18-year-old Brian was bruised and confused. He was unsure of how the car had veered off the road, and police officers called to the scene at first thought that he might have been under the influence of drugs or alcohol. Witnesses told paramedics that the vehicle was keeping up with traffic in the middle lane at 1:30 A.M. Although not many people were on the road at that time, a witness in a car behind Brian's noticed that his car had begun to weave slightly, but seemed to regain stability after a few seconds. The witness told the police that he thought that the driver might have been texting or talking on a cell phone or choosing a radio station. After five minutes, Brian's car began to weave more frequently, sharply drifting, and narrowly missing the car in the right lane. Surrounding cars began honking. Brian's car began to accelerate, driving over the curb, onto the sidewalk and crashing into a power pole. When bystanders approached, they found Brian conscious and confused, his face bloodied by glass shards from the vehicle's broken windshield. After police had determined that he was not under the influence of alcohol, he was transported to the nearest hospital, for further testing and treatment.

Upon admission into the hospital, Brian was still confused; he did not remember getting into the vehicle and starting his 30-minute trip. He admitted that he had stayed up almost all night for several nights before the accident with friends, studying for final exams. He was

11

exhausted, but the exams were so important to his final grades that he continued to force himself to remain awake. The night before the exam, he wanted to get a good night's sleep and wake up refreshed. Remembering that his mother had taken sleep medications in the past, he checked the medicine cabinet and found a prescription nonbenzodiazepine sleeping medication. Figuring that it would be out of his system in time for school the next morning, he took the pill and went to bed. Doctors concluded that the pill had caused him to hallucinate, and to "sleep drive," two of the potential side effects of this medication.

After the accident, Brian still could not believe that he had driven his car while asleep. As a result of the accident, Brian researched sleep medications on the Internet. He learned about the phases of the sleep cycle and the possible effects of taking certain sedative-hypnotic drugs, especially ones that had not been prescribed for him. Now, before exams, he tried to maintain a stable sleep schedule—no more trying to keep his body awake for a long period of time. If he must stay awake for a longer time, in conjunction with his doctor's instructions, instead of taking a drug that may interact with his sleep stages, he takes a mild medication that helps his body to start the sleep process.

Feeling tired is a familiar part of daily teenage life. With work, school, sports, lessons, and fun eating up the hours in a day and much of the night, sleep often takes a backseat. Since the body uses nighttime sleep as a way to regenerate the systems that keep energy flowing and the brain functioning at maximum levels during the day, it is important to give the most popular nighttime activity—sleeping—the respect and attention that it deserves.

Depriving the body of sleep creates tired, cranky, depressed teens. Shifting sleep schedules also create troubles in falling asleep and staying asleep. A seemingly easy route to dreamland for some involves taking over-the-counter or prescription sleep medications. Experimentation with drugs can start early. *Prescription for Danger*, a report published by the Office of National Drug Control Policy, noted that among teens, 13 is the mean age of first nonprescribed use of sedatives and stimulants. Prescription drugs most commonly abused by teens are painkillers, depressants such as sleeping pills or anti-anxiety drugs, and stimulants, mainly prescribed to treat **attention-deficit/hyperactivity disorder** (ADHD). Nearly one-third of teens (31%) believe there's "nothing wrong" with using prescription medicines without a prescription once in a while. Prescribed medications are not thought of as risky "street drugs," even if they are not prescribed to the person who takes them. The majority of teens who abuse these products get them for free, usually from friends and relatives, and often without their knowledge. Because of their easy availability, teens who otherwise would not touch street drugs might abuse prescription drugs.[1] "The explosion in the prescription of addictive **opioids**, depressants and stimulants has, for many children, made their parents' medicine cabinet a greater temptation and threat than a street drug dealer," said Joseph A. Califano, Jr., the chairman and president of the National Center on Addiction and Substance Abuse at Columbia University.[2]

The teenage years are usually a time of experimentation and discovery. With drugs, however, experimentation can be unhealthy, and even life threatening. Because sleep medications were intended to treat different types of sleep disorders, they were formulated to affect the brain and other parts of the body in various ways. The consequences of taking sleep or relaxation medications without a doctor's recommendations can be serious. Drugs that interact with the brain and the central nervous system, even in small doses, can affect thinking and motor skills that may increase the risk of injury, particularly during sports activities or driving. From a longer-term perspective, the brains of teenagers are still developing, and the effects of drug abuse may be harmful in ways that are not yet understood.[3]

IN SEARCH OF SLEEP

Whether prescription or over-the-counter, taking a medication to help start the sleep process without a doctor's guidance can yield unexpected, and maybe unwanted, results. For example, drugs usually taken for allergies or the common cold contain a chemical called diphenhydramine, which is an **antihistamine**. **Histamines** are brain chemicals that control wakefulness, so their antihistamine relatives encourage sleepiness. Over-the-counter sleep medications, such as Sominex and Nytol, contain similar, if not the exactly the same, chemicals. Some sleep aids mix the antihistamine with other ingredients, such as acetaminophen or alcohol. While these medications do not seem potentially harmful, they are not meant for long-term use, due to side effects such as confusion, next-day drowsiness, and potential for addiction.

The brain plays a big role in sleep. Some prescription medications, known as **sedative-hypnotics**, promote calmness and encourage sleepiness by working with the brain and central nervous system to either get people to sleep or help them stay asleep. Not all sleep medications work the same way. **Benzodiazepines**, one of the older group of medications in this category, may lose their effectiveness after continued use, causing people to feel like they need a stronger dose to achieve the same results. This is called "**tolerance**." Some newer medications, called non-benzodiazepines, have fewer side effects, but they still can cause morning grogginess, headaches, dizziness, nausea, sleepwalking (or sleep driving) and **rebound insomnia**, a condition that makes it even harder for the person to fall asleep after the pill wears off. Other sleep drugs are formulated to work in different ways. A relatively newer medication, containing the chemical ramelteon (Rozerem), imitates the sleep regulation hormone **melatonin**. It may help a person fall asleep, but it is not intended to help the person stay asleep. Side effects of this drug are dizziness and depression. Some antidepressants induce sleep, although this category is not recommended for sleep problems. For children and adolescents, these drugs carry an increased risk for suicidal thoughts or worsening of depression.[4]

Some people use medications prescribed for other medical conditions for their sleep-creating side effects. Opioids containing chemicals usually used to relieve pain are also taken by those who are trying to get a good night's rest. From one of the most common forms in the opium family, **codeine**, to more potent forms such as **morphine**, the nonmedical use of prescription opioids has increased significantly among adolescents and young adults during the past decade in the United States. More than 1 in every 10 high school seniors reported nonmedical use of prescription opioids.[5] Women reported higher prevalence rates than men using this drug to get to sleep. Because of the way this drug interacts with other medications or alcohol, using these drugs to get to sleep can be very dangerous, even life threatening.

Some sleep medications and supplements contain body chemicals like melatonin or herbal ingredients that are thought to cause sleep. Even though they are sold in health food stores and over-the-counter, they still can have a physical effect on the body, when taken alone or with other medications, so anyone who wants to take them should discuss their use with a doctor.

Figure 1.1 When used according to directions and under a doctor's care, sleep medications can help someone with a sleep disorder to achieve a restful night's sleep. (© Alamy)

SLEEP DISORDERS

Sleep disorders in younger people are very common and, in their most extreme forms, can interfere with daily functioning by producing emotional and behavioral problems as well as hindering thought processes. Sleep disorders earlier in life are classified in the following three categories: **dyssomnias**, or difficulty starting or maintaining sleep; **parasomnias**, or disruption of existing sleep; and medical-psychiatric disorders, or other medical conditions that include sleep problems. These three categories include the sleep disorders that teens may experience because of their lifestyle, body changes during this time in life, or because of pre-existing physical conditions.[6]

Many common sleep disorders are contained in the dyssomnia category. **Delayed sleep phase syndrome**, in which people try for several hours to fall asleep, is very common among teens, with about 7% of adolescents diagnosed with this condition. **Narcolepsy**, characterized by episodes of suddenly falling asleep and falls during the day, and feelings of **paralysis** during sleep, is frustrating and embarrassing, but treatable. Sleep **apnea**, which involves pauses in breathing during sleep, and movement-related disorders such as **restless legs syndrome** (RLS) and periodic limb movements in sleep (PLMS) also cause difficulty in getting to sleep and obtaining a peaceful night's sleep.

Parasomnias, including sleepwalking, nightmares, and **night terrors**, are not only frightening, but dangerous. These sleep disorders can result in people awakening to find that they have eaten a whole bag of candy or even driven a car.

Medical-psychiatric disorders result from other physical conditions that include sleep problems as well. Examples of these include hyperactivity

STUDYING WITH YOUR EYES CLOSED

Cramming for a test while awake is tough enough, but there are some people who have suggested that listening to a recorded message or facts while sleeping will help the information "seep" into the brain. Matthew Walker, director of the Sleep and Neuroimaging Lab at Beth Israel Deaconess Medical Center and assistant professor of psychology at Harvard Medical School, says that learning definitely works much better when the learner is awake. He explains that during sleep, the brain focuses internally on what it learned during the day, rather than sounds and happenings externally, such as a recorded message. So what's the best way to get the brain ready for the cram session? He suggests getting a full night of sleep the day before intense studying so the brain will be relaxed and receptive. During the following day, put the brain in high gear by thinking about and trying to understand the material. Get a full night's sleep afterward so the information can become part of your memory bank.

Source: "Sleep: Expert Q&A," Nova (PBS), http://www.pbs.org/wgbh/nova/body/walker-sleep.html (accessed January 19, 2011).

disorders that could cause RLS, PLMS, or sleep apnea. Me■ affect sleep, as can anxiety, stress, and depression.

Teens who abuse substances such as alcohol, amphe cocaine, opioids, sedatives, hypnotics, or anxiety-reducin₵ develop sleep disorders. Over time, as the body gets used ᴛᴏ ᴛʜᴇ ᴅʀᴜɢs, ᴛʜᴇ person not only needs an increased dose to get the same effect, but the drug may also cause sleep problems. In addition to sleep problems caused by taking these substances, sleep can also be interfered with during the withdrawal period from these drugs.

HOW SLEEP WORKS

Understanding the sleep process can be an eye-opener. Everyone has a 24-hour internal clock, called circadian rhythm, that influences such biological and psychological processes as sleep cycles, body temperature, appetite, and hormonal changes. The main part of the clock that controls **circadian rhythms** is a group of nerve cells in the brain called the **suprachiasmatic nucleus**, or SCN. The clock responds primarily to light and darkness in the environment, and since the SCN is located above the optic nerves, the natural connection between light, dark, and sleep becomes more apparent. Most living things, even plants and animals, have circadian rhythms. These circadian rhythms urge younger children to fall asleep usually around 8 or 9 P.M., but changes in body chemistry during puberty delay this natural sleep signal until about 11 P.M. or even later.[7]

Body chemicals also are an important part of the sleep mix. A chemical messenger called **adenosine** combined with the circadian clock sends signals to the body that it is time for sleep.

Adenosine builds up in the blood during the day as the body uses energy. When the brain detects that adenosine has reached certain levels, the person begins to feel sleepy. During sleep, enzymes break down the adenosine, reducing the levels. As a result of this process, the longer people stay awake, the sleepier they feel.[8]

Sleep is also induced by the natural hormone melatonin, produced in the brain by the body's **pineal gland**.[9] The pineal gland takes a break during the day, but it works the night shift, producing melatonin and releasing it into the blood. The SCN controls melatonin production. When melatonin levels

, alertness decreases. During the dark hours, the SCN sends the brain a message to make more melatonin, which causes drowsiness. Melatonin levels in the blood stay elevated through the night and reduce as daytime approaches.

Sleep researcher Mary Carskadon examined melatonin secretion to explore this chemical's effect on teen sleep. She discussed research on 10 adolescents with a mean age of 13.7, who were put on a fixed sleeping schedule for 10 days at home and then in a laboratory. A connection was found between the participants' melatonin secretion and their stage of development: Melatonin onset occurs later in adolescents, making it difficult for them to go to sleep earlier at night. At the same time, the hormone "turns off" later in the morning, making it harder for them to wake up early.[10]

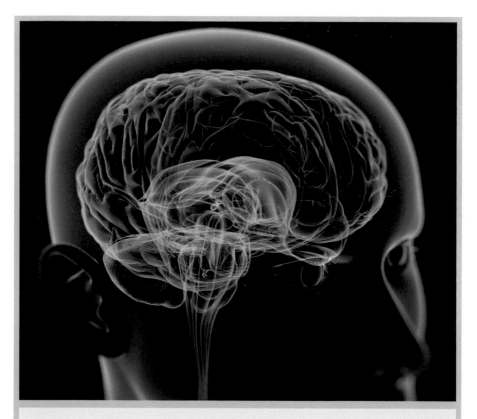

Figure 1.2 Melatonin, a natural hormone produced in the brain by the body's pineal gland, induces sleep. (© *Photo Researchers*)

THE STAGES OF SLEEP

While hormones are hard at work while a person sleeps, the body also is hard at work to ensure a good night's rest. Five basic stages are involved with the natural cycles of brain activity during sleep. The first four stages, each lasting from 5 to 15 minutes, are called **non-Rapid Eye Movement (NREM) sleep**. The last stage of sleep is **Rapid Eye Movement (REM) sleep**. These phases are repeated, in order, up to about five times each night.

- Stage 1—This stage can feel like "drowsiness," and can last 5 to 10 minutes. The eyes are closed, muscle activity slows, and the eyes move under the eyelids. It is easy to be awakened during this stage, and if that happens, the person may not even think that he/she had fallen asleep at all.
- Stage 2 –During this light sleep phase, eye movements stop, heart rate slows, body temperature decreases, and the body prepares for some serious sleeping.
- Stages 3 and 4—When awakened during these deep sleep phases, a person may feel groggy and confused. Since the brain does not need as much blood while the body is resting, blood flow is redirected to the muscles, to help refresh physical energy.
- Stage 5—About 60 to 90 minutes after falling asleep, the body enters the fifth and final stage, REM sleep. During this stage, the eyes move quickly, darting in different directions, and heart rate and respiration speed up and become irregular. Brain activity increases, but many voluntary muscles experience a type of paralysis in the arms and legs. Intense dreaming occurs during REM sleep, and this paralysis stops the body from actually carrying out the physical movements occurring in our dreams. Without this paralysis, a dream about sky-diving could result in a jump out the window, or a dream about running a marathon could cause the dreamer to run into a wall.

Often, people deprived of REM sleep cannot remember something that they studied before falling asleep.[11] Changing the sleep pattern or depriving the body of sleep can be harmful and interfere with the process of thinking and learning. REM sleep stimulates the part of the brain used for learning.

It is important to get a good night's sleep because the body needs this phase to repair tissues, build bone and muscle, and strengthen the **immune system**, processes that help the body to stay healthy, avoid illnesses, and fight bacteria and viruses and other infection-producers.[12] A graphic example of sleep deprivation and its consequences in teenagers was reported by Eve van Cauter from the University of Chicago. When students were allowed to sleep only four hours per night for six nights, their bodies rebelled. When they received a flu vaccine, their immune systems produced half the normal number of antibodies to fight the virus; their levels of **cortisol** (also known as the stress hormone) rose; their **sympathetic nervous system** became active, raising heart rate and blood pressure; they showed **insulin resistance** that

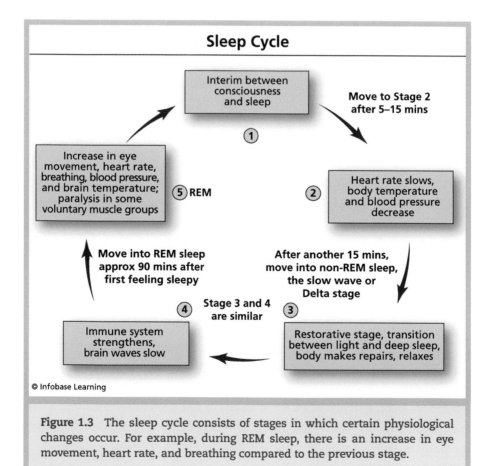

Sleep Cycle

Interim between consciousness and sleep ①

Move to Stage 2 after 5–15 mins

⑤ REM — Increase in eye movement, heart rate, breathing, blood pressure, and brain temperature; paralysis in some voluntary muscle groups

② Heart rate slows, body temperature and blood pressure decrease

Move into REM sleep approx 90 mins after first feeling sleepy

After another 15 mins, move into non-REM sleep, the slow wave or Delta stage

④ Stage 3 and 4 are similar ③

Immune system strengthens, brain waves slow

Restorative stage, transition between light and deep sleep, body makes repairs, relaxes

© Infobase Learning

Figure 1.3 The sleep cycle consists of stages in which certain physiological changes occur. For example, during REM sleep, there is an increase in eye movement, heart rate, and breathing compared to the previous stage.

potentially could affect **glucose tolerance** and produce weight gain; and they showed reduced levels of **leptin**, a substance secreted by fat cells to curb appetite. The sleep researcher noted that if kept on a sleep-deprived schedule such as during the test, within a couple of weeks an 18-year-old could exhibit the same ability to metabolize glucose as a 60-year-old. That is a problem, especially since junk food cravings are also a result of sleep deprivation.[13]

Because of the importance of giving each phase of sleep the time that it needs for the body and mind to reset, repair and relax, interfering with the process can result in trouble remembering and thinking, depression, and increased probability of getting sick.

STATS ON SLEEP

Because of the body's reaction to lack of sleep, it is important to understand that tiredness can present a hazard in the driver's seat. A National Sleep Foundation Sleep in America poll in 2006 showed that more than half of teens drove drowsy in the year before the study, and 15% of drivers in 10th to 12th grades said that they drove drowsy at least once a week.[14] Sometimes lack of sleep is beyond the teen's control. A study in Virginia, conducted in conjunction with the Virginia Department of Motor Vehicles, studied drivers between 16 years old and 18 years old in two counties with differing school start times: in Virginia Beach, where high schools start at 7:20 A.M., and in Chesapeake, where high schools start at 8:40 A.M. Results showed that the students who started earlier were involved in 65.4 car crashes for every 1,000 teen drivers. In comparison, Chesapeake County showed 46.2 crashes per 1,000 teen drivers, a 40% lower crash rate than at the earlier school.[15] School officials are learning from these statistics and trying to change school start times to reduce sleep-related accidents.

Lack of sleep also affects schoolwork. Results of a 2010 study presented at SLEEP 2010, the 24th Annual Meeting of the Associated Professional Sleep Societies, indicate that moderate to severe obstructive sleep apnea was linked to both lower academic grades and behavioral problems.[16] Tests at Harvard Medical School and at Trent University in Canada show that the brain consolidates and practices skills or information learned by day during certain phases of sleep. Dr. Robert Stickgold of Harvard University Medical

TOO TIRED TO DRIVE?

An AAA Foundation survey showed that 9 out of 10 police officers reported stopping a driver whom they believed was drunk but turned out to be drowsy. Improper sleep habits affect people of all ages. The American Academy of Sleep Medicine noted that 80,000 individuals fall asleep at the wheel each day, and there are more than 250,000 sleep-related motor vehicle accidents each year. Their data show that 20% of all serious transportation injuries on U.S. highways are related to sleep. Although teenagers often get less sleep than adults, they really need more sleep—about nine hours a night to be fully rested.

Without enough sleep, the body may resort to catching short naps called **microsleeps** that can last just a few seconds, so short that the person may not even be aware that this is happening. Micro-sleeps occur with no advance warning, and response time is severely reduced. Adding just a small amount of sleep to the schedule can keep danger out of the driver's seat.

Here are some warning signs of drowsy driving:

- Trouble focusing, keeping eyes open, or holding head up
- Yawning or rubbing your eyes repeatedly
- Daydreaming and wandering thoughts
- Slower reaction time, poor judgment
- Drifting from the lane, tailgating and missing signs or exits
- Turning up the radio or rolling down the window
- Trouble remembering landmarks that were passed or time spent driving

Source: National Sleep Foundation and AAA Foundation for Traffic Safety

School found that the amount of certain brain chemicals is reduced during the beginning of the night, while information flows out of the **hippocampus** (the memory region) and into the **cortex** (region of awareness, thought, and language).[17] After that, the brain distributes the new information into its different areas to organize and categorize it efficiently and then to integrate it. Brain proteins work to fortify connections between nerve cells to reinforce new information learned the day before. Then, during Rapid Eye Movement (REM) sleep (the fifth stage of sleep), the brain reenacts the lessons learned the day before and deposits them in the brain's memory banks.

Even if parents spend a lot of time nagging their teens to maintain good sleep habits, teens cannot take all of the blame for lack of sleep. In the teenage "**biological clock**" lurks a tendency to fall asleep later and to wake up later, known as "**sleep phase delay**." A sleep study by researchers Mary Carskadon and William C. Dement showed that when teenagers were deprived of sleep, their daytime sleepiness increased. However, even with restricted sleep the night before, the students still reported feeling more energetic the following evening, which allowed them to stay up late, even past midnight. The researchers also found that the effects of lost sleep accumulate, and this "**sleep debt**" increases the negative consequences over time.[18]

2
History of Sleep Drugs

Strange things had been happening to Robert during the past few months. It all started at college when the stress of the classes and his part-time job and the noise of the dorm all made it hard for him to fall asleep. He usually was tired all day, and by the time he got finished with classes, socialized a bit, had some dinner and was back in his room, he got a "second wind," a burst of energy that kept him awake until 2 A.M. or sometimes even later. Even when he tried to get to bed early, his mind was active, thinking of all he had to do the next day. Even though Robert kept a very similar schedule to his friends', his sleep schedule bothered him. Even when he did finally get to sleep, he would wake often, thinking of a detail of the fraternity party that needed to be attended to, or trying to remember if he locked the back door of the pizza store where he worked when he left that night.

Finally, Robert went to the doctor and discussed how to regulate his sleep. The doctor at first suggested that Robert create a more relaxing bedtime routine and minimize distractions—an impossibility for life in the dorm as far as Robert was concerned. So, the doctor prescribed a sleep medication in the sedative-hypnotic category. Robert began taking the medication as prescribed and found that he was sleeping more consistently and longer during the night. Then, things started to happen that Robert blamed on his roommates. One day, he bought a box of his favorite cookies to take with him to class, and the next morning the box was empty. He yelled at his roommates and accused them of stealing the cookies. They denied taking the cookies, and he couldn't understand why they would lie when they had been friends for so long. This happened several times in the next few weeks. He would wake up to find empty food containers in the room, and he continued to be frustrated and upset. Why would they take his food and be shameless enough to leave the empty box right by his bedside?

Then Robert's suspicion turned to worry. Robert's sister, Lisa, called him one day to tell him that although she didn't mind helping him with this physics homework, she really would appreciate if he would not call her in the middle of the night. She explained that his call had awakened her out of a deep sleep, but she chatted for a few minutes anyway, thinking that maybe Robert wanted to discuss a family matter or girlfriend problem. Again, Robert was confused. He had not called Lisa, and told her that his buddies had been playing pranks on him by stealing his snacks but he never thought that they would stoop to prank calling his sister in the middle of the night and impersonating him! She insisted that it was his voice that she heard, but Robert said that he had taken his sleeping pill and been fast asleep all night.

A few weeks later, Robert found out that the cookie bandit and the midnight caller were not his friends playing pranks. He took his sleeping pill and went to sleep. He was dreaming of a long, relaxing drive along the beach with a beautiful girl in the passenger seat. Then he was jolted out of his dream by a loud siren and glaring, blinking red and blue lights. He squinted, trying to see who was shining a flashlight in his face. He was confused and groggy but was sitting behind the wheel of his car. The police were telling him to get out of the car, asking if he was out drinking, or if he was on drugs. They took him back to the police station, where he awoke the next morning, very surprised to find that he was not in his bed in the dorm.

To his surprise, Robert found out that he had been "sleep driving." He had no memory of getting out of bed, getting into the car, or driving down the road and stopping on a baseball field. Luckily, it was so late at night that not many people were out on the road. No one was hurt, and Robert was not charged, since he had taken a prescription medication and did not take any other drugs or drink alcohol with it. After apologizing to his friends, Robert decided to take a sleep study and see if he could find a different way to tackle his sleep issues. He also decided *to put his car keys in a different spot before going to sleep, and give his cookies to his friends for safekeeping.*

SLEEPLESS IN SUMERIA

For thousands of years, **insomnia**, or continuing sleeplessness, has harassed both young and old alike. Long before scientists began mixing chemicals in laboratories, people used Mother Nature's flowers and herbs to calm the nerves, relax the body, or relieve the mind of stressful thoughts enough to get a good night's rest. One of the earliest and most popular sleep medications was **opium**, which is made from the seed of the opium flower. Author Martin Bloom notes in his book *Opium: A History*, that as early as 3400 B.C., the Sumerians called opium poppies "the joy plant" because of its calming effects. The plant was also used by the Assyrians, the Babylonians, and Egyptians.[1] Opium's legendary sleep-causing powers were so great that even sleepless gods were believed to use it for divine rest. The Greek god of sleep, Hypnos, the Roman god of sleep, Somnus, and the Minoan goddess of sleep all have been portrayed carrying opium pods or wearing a crown of the colorful blooms. Traders carried the poppies to India and China, countries that eventually began growing their own poppy crops. Besides the potent poppy, ancient Greek and Roman doctors used various natural sleep inducers such as bark of mandrake, or mandragora, the seeds of an herb called henbane, and even lettuce juice. During the Middle Ages in Europe, a sleep remedy called *spongia somnifera* was used; it consisted of sponges soaked in wine and various herbs. In England, similar syrupy insomnia remedies were called "drowsy syrups."

FLOWER POWER

In 1803 a German scientist, Frederick Serturner, cooked up a new drug by extracting and purifying the active ingredients in opium. The recipe produced a substance that was 10 times stronger than opium. He named it morphine, after the Greek god of dreams, Morpheus.[2] Another opium-based compound, **codeine**, was discovered in 1832. These medications are very effective for calming nerves and causing sleep, but these **opiate** drugs (derived from opium) have been highly abused over the years. In fact, by 1900 approximately 1 million Americans had developed a dependency.[3] Just a few of the negative side effects of opiates include: drowsiness, mental clouding, breathing problems, itching, nausea, vomiting, and drop in blood pressure.

KO, NOT OK

Besides opium, two sleep-inducing drugs used in the nineteenth century were chloral hydrate and bromides. Easier to take than a pill, chloral hydrate is available in liquid syrup, soft capsule form, or rectal suppositories. It takes effect in about 30 minutes, with sleep occurring in about 60 minutes. After its discovery in the early 1830s, chloral hydrate quickly began to be abused. It has been misued by mixing it in drinks, resulting in its nicknames of "knockout drops" or a "Mickey Finn." (Mickey Finn was the owner of a saloon in Chicago during the early 1900s who was rumored to have drugged and robbed his customers.) Combining this drug with alcohol or another type of sleep medication is extremely dangerous and potentially fatal.[4]

Bromides are another type of calming drug used in the second half of the nineteenth century. Bromides also presented problems, such as irritability, hallucinations, delirium, and lethargy. They could stay in a user's system for about 12 days, so they became unpopular, and yet another category of drug, barbiturates, gained favor in the early part of the twentieth century[5]

THE TRUTH ABOUT TRUTH SERUM

The first barbiturate, barbital, introduced in 1903, encouraged sleep and eased anxiety; by 1912, an anticonvulsive ingredient was added, making phenobarbitol. This type of drug became so popular that about 20 different barbiturates were developed. One barbiturate that became well known thanks to spy and mystery movies is sodium pentothal—known by its nickname, "truth serum." Although sodium pentothal may lower inhibitions and make a person more talkative, taking it really does not "force" a person to tell the truth. The problem with barbiturates is that the effects change depending on the amount taken. In low doses, barbiturates reduce anxiety, breathing rate, blood pressure, and heart rate, and reduce Rapid Eye Movement (REM) sleep. It may sound reasonable that a larger dose would do the same as a smaller dose—just more so—that is definitely not the case. In higher doses, barbiturates can actually stimulate the body functions.

A major problem with barbiturates is their potential to create tolerance in frequent users. With consistent use, a person may discover that he or she needs a higher dose of the drug to get same effect. These drugs also cause dependence: The user feels that she or he must have it, and experiences a bad physical reaction when he or she stops taking it, such as anxiety, trouble sleeping, seizures, nausea, stomach problems, and hallucinations. Even more dangerous, the effective dose of this drug is close to the lethal dose, so barbiturates taken incorrectly can result in accidental death.[6] By the 1980s the popularity of barbituates decreased as more people became aware of their disadvantages.[7]

THE GOOD, THE BAD, AND THE SLEEPY

After more people became aware of the hazards of barbiturates, benzodiazepines became the sleep medication of choice. By the 1980s they were the most prescribed medicines in America.[8] At first these were thought to be safer and less habit-forming than barbiturates. However, because of their calming effects, benzodiazepines have a high potential for abuse, especially when taken with other depressants such as alcohol or opiates. Common brand names are Xanax, Librium, Valium, and Ativan. Rohypnol has made news headlines under the nickname "the date rape drug." These drugs are intended to relax, calm, and relieve tension, but they can also have bad side effects, such as impaired motor coordination, drowsiness, fatigue, indifference, impaired memory, confusion, and depression, to name just a few. In high doses, benzodiazepines can cause slow reflexes, mood swings, and hostility.

THE SPELL OF SEDATIVE-HYPNOTICS

Another type of drug, non-benzodiazepines, was developed to treat the symptoms of sleep disorders while reducing the tolerance and addiction issues associated with benzodiazepines. These drugs, which include zolpidem (Ambien), eszopiclone (Lunesta), and zaleplon (Sonata), are called **sedative-hypnotics**—*sedative* for calming and *hypnotic* for causing sleep. Because most of them start with the letter Z, they are nicknamed "Z-drugs." People can become addicted to or develop a tolerance to these drugs. Non-benzodiazepines also interfere with REM sleep. REM sleep is associated with dreaming. Because of this, sedative-hypnotics can have disturbing side effects. In some cases, people have been known to drive cars, eat, and make phone calls while sleeping.

From the earliest times to now, sleep medications have been both a blessing and curse. When used for medical purposes, they can give virtually anyone—including teenagers—a proper night's sleep, a better attitude, and more energy during the day. Even with their positive results, the possibilities exist for abuse. Because so many new drugs appear on the market each day, it is impossible for the average teenager or parent to keep current on all of the possible bad effects. That is why governmental departments such as the U.S. Food and Drug Administration (FDA) demand that these companies give guiding principles to people who will be taking these drugs legally.

ABUSED OR JUST USED?

To determine if a drug has the potential for abuse, the Controlled Substances Act asks questions like these to establish a drug's potential for abuse.

- Is there evidence that that the drug or other substance can be taken in amounts large enough to create a hazard to their health or to the safety of other individuals or to the community?
- Are people getting the drug from legitimate drug channels such as the drug store, hospital or doctor, or is it coming from someone on the street or in a school?
- Do people take the drug or other substance on their own rather than with medical advice from a person licensed by law (such as a doctor or pharmacist) to administer such drug?
- If the drug is new, is it related in action to a drug or other substance already listed as having a potential for abuse? Is it likely that the drug will have the same potential for abuse as the related drug?

Source: U.S. Drug Enforcement Administration

IMPORTANT INSTRUCTIONS

To warn people of the risks of these medications, the FDA requested in early 2007 that all manufacturers of sedative-hypnotic drug products strengthen their product labeling to include warnings about complex sleep-related behaviors and other reactions, such as the life-threatening full-body reactions known as **anaphylaxis** and hive-like swelling called **angioedema**. The reactions were so widespread that the FDA also requested that manufacturers of sedative-hypnotic products send letters to health care providers to notify them about the new warnings. The companies also must develop Patient Medication Guides to be given to patients, their families, or caregivers when the medication is prescribed, to inform them about risks and advise them of precautions and consequences for mixing these medications with other drugs or alcohol. Drug manufacturers also must conduct clinical studies to investigate how often sleep-driving and other complex behaviors occur in association with their drug products.[9]

TOUGH SCHEDULE

As long as 40 years ago, the government began to take a watchdog role over drugs and other harmful substances and their possible abuses. According to the U.S. Drug Enforcement Administration, the Controlled Substances Act (CSA), Title II and Title III of the Comprehensive Drug Abuse Prevention and Control Act of 1970, is a combination of many laws regulating the manufacture and distribution of narcotics, stimulants, depressants, hallucinogens, anabolic steroids, and chemicals used in the illegal production of controlled substances.

The CSA places certain regulated substances on five "schedules" based on the substance's medical use, potential for abuse, and safety or potential for dependence. It is very difficult to figure out if a drug is going to harm someone. To determine which schedule a drug or other substance should be placed in, or whether a drug should not be controlled at all or should be rescheduled, certain factors must be considered, such as the drug's actual or relative potential for abuse; the science of the drug, including its composition, uses, and effects; current scientific knowledge about the substance; history and current pattern of abuse; information on risk to the public health; discussion of whether the drug is physically addictive or habit forming; and whether the substance is related to a substance that is already controlled. After considering these factors, the administrator makes decisions about which schedule the drug belongs on.

Schedules establish a scale from number one, for the highest potential of abuse, to number five, for the lowest. The highest are not currently accepted for medical use in treatment in the United States. Schedule I and II drugs include heroin, marijuana, methaqualone, morphine, cocaine, methadone and methamphetamine. Schedule III drugs have less potential for abuse and have a currently accepted medical use in treatment in the United States, such as codeine and hydrocodone with aspirin or acetaminophen (Tylenol), and some barbiturates. Schedule IV drugs, some of which are used for sleep disorders, have a currently accepted medical use in treatment in the United States, but when abused may lead to addiction. These include such drugs as pentazocine (Talwin), meprobamate (Equanil), diazepam (Valium), zolpidem (Ambien), zaleplon (Sonata), and alprazolam (Xanax). Schedule V drugs have low potential for abuse, such as cough medicines with codeine.[10]

Whatever the drug schedule, everyone must be very careful to take sleep medication according to the doctors' orders or, at the very least, according to the instructions on the label. Because of their effects, mixing sleep medications with alcohol or other drugs can lead to hospitalization or, worse, death. When medications are taken correctly, they can help to ease the frustration and anxiety of a daily schedule that does not include enough sleep.

3
Sleep Disorders

When Miriam heard her classmates complain that they could not fall asleep at night, she wondered if they would understand her problem. She had no problems going to sleep, but during the day, Miriam could fall asleep anywhere—at her desk, in the cafeteria, even waiting for her turn during a swim meet. Her frustration grew as her acquaintances started to make fun of her, her teachers lectured her to pay attention, and her friends began to lose patience when she fell asleep during their conversations.

It was bad enough to endure the unscheduled daytime naps, but Miriam also began to experience **hallucinations** *right before going to sleep at night. She "saw" dolls on her shelf wink at her, and even "heard" them ask her if they could come to school with her the next day. One morning, she woke up but felt that she was unable to move. She tried to call for help, but couldn't formulate the words. She had to concentrate as hard as she could to even wiggle one tiny toe. Feeling unable to breathe, she started to panic. This only lasted a few seconds, but felt like much longer.*

When she told her parents, they said that she was probably going through a phase and that she should get to bed earlier. They also dismissed her hallucinations as "bad dreams," although they seemed so realistic to Miriam. She started to doubt her own sanity and become depressed. Feeling that she must take the situation into her own hands, Miriam went to the supermarket and bought some over-the-counter "stay awake" medicine. It helped somewhat, but not quite enough, and during the next few weeks, she began to increase the amount that she took each day.

At lunch in the school cafeteria, Miriam confided in a friend that she needed help staying awake and that she wished she could get some stronger pills. The friend suggested that she try a drug used to treat attention-deficit/hyperactivity disorder, a condition that makes it difficult to concentrate. She said that it would make her feel more energetic. Miriam's friend knew someone who had a prescription and would be able to sell her some, on a regular basis. Thinking that a doctor wouldn't issue a prescription unless the drug was fairly safe, Miriam agreed. She began to take the drug each day, increasing the dose when she felt that she needed the extra concentration that the pills provided, such as on test days. When it seemed like they helped, she took more. On days when she didn't have the money to buy enough, or she forgot, Miriam felt depressed, crying for hours. She started to feel sick to her stomach much of the time.

The school nurse called her parents when Miriam came to her office shaking uncontrollably. Her blood pressure was high, and her heart was pounding. Crying, she told the nurse that in the past few months she had taken both over-the-counter and prescription drugs to stay awake, sometimes even mixing the two. She told the nurse about her hallucinations and her feeling of paralysis and how she would fall asleep even when interested in a conversation or activity. The nurse said she didn't think Miriam was crazy, and recommended that Miriam be tested by a doctor who specializes in sleep disorders.

After testing, the doctor discovered that Miriam had narcolepsy. After going through a period of rehabilitation to treat the depression caused by the pills, she was able to get the medication that she actually needed, and regulate it in the right dosage. She also began to make lifestyle changes, like minimizing caffeine intake and exploring her own sleep habits to find out the sleep schedule that her body needed. Although Miriam's narcolepsy cannot be cured, it is now controlled. She is happy to report that she breathes more freely at night now, and when she says goodnight to her dolls on the shelf, they no longer say anything back.

Getting a good night's sleep seems like a simple enough task. Just work hard all day, jump into bed, and drift off into dreamland when the head hits the pillow. For many teenagers, that is an unlikely and unachievable scenario. According to the National Institute of Neurological Disorders and Stroke, doctors have noted more than 70 sleep disorders.[1] For teenagers, sleep is important, but often work, school, and socializing get in the way of sleeping for the right number of hours and under the right circumstances. A workshop entitled Sleep Needs, Patterns, and Difficulties of Adolescents was held on September 22, 1999, so that policy makers, researchers, and doctors could examine adolescence and sleep. William C. Dement, a pioneer in the field of sleep research, explained, "Adolescence is the time of greatest vulnerability from the standpoint of sleep."[2] Sleep patterns that do not promote a good night's sleep are often accepted as a natural part of the teenage years. Researchers of teen sleep have repeatedly shown that while the need for sleep does not decrease during adolescence, the amount of sleep that adolescents get drops, causing chronic problems.

Some sleep disorders are more common than others during the teenage years. Catching them early can prevent lifelong sleep issues. These disorders have real symptoms, side effects, and treatment. While some people depend on behavior changes for solutions, some need medications to help regain control of sleep patterns.

INSOMNIA

Teenagers live in a world of high activity and change. Studying, extracurricular activities, socialization, and work keep this age group on the go for much of the day and often into the night. While outside responsibilities contribute to the hectic schedule, changes in brain activity during this time alter sleep patterns established during childhood. **Insomnia**, chronic or reoccurring inability to sleep, is common during adolescence, but for many the solution is more complicated than just getting to bed earlier. The consequences of losing too much sleep are serious. A study at the University of Texas indicated that teenagers who show symptoms of insomnia are more likely than other teens to develop depression or problems with substance abuse or to entertain thoughts of suicide by the time they reach early adulthood.[3]

Sleep problems that are unrelated to health problems are categorized as **primary insomnia**. This is caused by prolonged stress, travel, or work or school schedules that interfere with sleep. Even though primary insomnia can be caused by a temporary event, the effects can be long lasting. The body may find it hard to kick bad sleep habits that were formed during the crisis, such as napping or worrying before bedtime.[4] **Secondary insomnia** results

Figure 3.1 Insomnia is a common condition involving chronic sleeplessness. (© *Photo Researchers*)

from health conditions (such as pain, asthma, depression, arthritis, cancer, or heartburn), medication, or use of other substances, such as alcohol.[5]

Besides the cause, the type of insomnia is also defined by the amount of time that it lasts. If the inability to sleep lasts for a short time, the condition is called **acute insomnia**, and if it lasts for a longer time (at least three nights a week for a month or longer), it is called **chronic insomnia**.

DELAYED SLEEP PHASE SYNDROME

Delayed sleep phase syndrome (DSPS) is one of the most common sleep disorders among teenagers. Busy schedules plus bodily changes that happen during puberty equal difficulty getting to sleep. People affected by DSPS can lie awake in bed trying to fall asleep for two to even four hours.

One of the lesser known body changes that happens during puberty is a shift in the teen's internal clock. This delays the desire to sleep by about two hours or even more. The "normal" teen schedule makes this even worse. Waking up to go to school at 7 A.M., and then either working or returning home to do homework, in addition to socializing, leaves little time for sleep during the week. This type of schedule already makes it difficult to wake up in the morning, but it also makes it tough to get to sleep at night. Teenagers usually get sleepy sometime during the afternoon, but in the evening get a "second wind" that keeps them up late into the night. On weekends, the schedule is even more sleepless. Partying late on Friday and Saturday nights usually results in sleeping late on Saturday and Sunday mornings. As a result of this constant shift in sleep habits, the body's internal clock is not only shifted more but also becomes quite confused.

While it may seem simple to advise someone with DSPS to just go to sleep earlier, that is easier to say than to do when the body clock is involved. The body feels as if it is in a state of constant jet lag—as though it were flying from California to New York and experiencing the time change from Pacific Standard Time to Eastern Standard Time every night. The mind knows what time it really is, yet the body's clock is set for another sleep zone.[6]

DSPS can cause daytime sleepiness, inability to fall asleep at night, and inability to wake up on time in the morning. Even if they get into bed at a proper bedtime, some teens lie awake for hours until falling asleep. This can be extremely frustrating, and can cause depression and other behavior problems as a result of the daytime sleepiness and nighttime wakefulness.

Because DSPS is encouraged by a teenager's busy schedule, it is difficult to treat. However, a motivated teen can regain a healthy sleep schedule by trying the many treatment options available.

Cultivating a better sleep environment is one way to bring consistency to the sleep schedule. This solution is difficult because inconsistency and change are part of everyday teen life. The first part of a regular sleep schedule is establishing a consistent time to go to bed and wake up every day. To accomplish this, teenagers need to avoid chemicals that would interfere with sleep, such as caffeine, cigarettes, or stimulating drugs. The bedroom should be "sleep friendly"—the proper temperature, quiet, and with a comfortable bed and pillows. Even though they may be enjoyable, stimulating television and computer games, exciting TV shows, and other action-oriented activities before bedtime are definitely banned from the bedroom.

A more complicated part of DSPS therapy is rescheduling the internal body clock. This takes time and patience. The body clock can be moved two ways, forward or backward. One method, moving the internal clock earlier, is called phase advancement. To start, move the bedtime fifteen minutes earlier for two nights (for example, from 12 A.M. to 11:45 P.M. for two nights, then to 11:30 for two nights, and so on) until the desired time for sleep is reached and achieved. Another technique is chronotherapy, or phase delay. For this more complicated therapy, the person needs to clear the schedule of school and work commitments because the sleep schedule is moved forward by 2 hours a day (gradually moving bedtime back through the day) until the desired bedtime is reached. For example, if the person usually falls asleep at 2 A.M., he or she delays sleep until 4 A.M. for a couple of days, and then stays up until 6 A.M. for a few days, and gradually moves the sleep time throughout the day, until the hour is reached at which they really want to go to sleep. Because of the amount of time, patience, and dedication needed for this approach, a sleep specialist or physician's help may be needed. Once a goal is reached by either of these phase methods, the teen must stick to the sleep schedule. It takes a very strong and motivated person to avoid late-night parties or study sessions to go home and get into bed. Getting off of the schedule, though, can result in returning to the sleepless nights.

Figure 3.2 Excessive daytime sleepiness may be a symptom of delayed sleep phase syndrome or narcolepsy. (© *Alamy*)

Since the body responds to morning and nighttime cues, such as sunshine and darkness, bright light therapy is another possibility. Using a special light box, the patient is exposed to a bright light in the morning for approximately 20 to 30 minutes, and stays away from bright light in the evening. This may help to coax the body into relaxation and then sleep, but there is an expense involved for the purchase of the light box.[7]

If these "natural" ways of regulating sleep are not enough to put the body back on the right sleep track, a pill containing melatonin, the hormone produced in the body that helps to regulate sleep patterns, may be indicated. For people with DSPS, the body releases melatonin at a later time than other people. Sometimes taking a small dose (1/2 milligram) of synthetic melatonin 5 to 7 hours before bedtime (in the late afternoon) can help shift the sleep cycle to an earlier time. This also should be done only under the care of a doctor.[8]

NARCOLEPSY

When a classmate makes a habit of falling asleep at his desk, narcolepsy may be source of the sudden snooze. Narcolepsy does more than just make someone miss some facts during class; it also interferes with daily life and safety. Normal sleep is divided into an organized pattern of REM (Rapid Eye Movement) and non-REM stages. Narcolepsy typically interrupts that pattern by awakening the person throughout the night. As a result, the REM sleep that is missed during the night can suddenly occur during the day, through hallucinations or sudden sleep. Narcoleptics may even involuntarily fall asleep at work or at school, in the middle of a conversation, while eating or, even worse, when driving.

Excessive daytime sleepiness (EDS) is the main symptom of narcolepsy. Because of the EDS, involuntary sleep episodes can last a few seconds at a time. The National Institute of Neurological Disorders and Stroke cites that "As many as 40% of all people with narcolepsy are prone to *automatic behavior* during such microsleeps, falling asleep for a few seconds while still carrying out a task. Afterward, people cannot recall their actions. In some cases, the person has the sensation of forgetting where he or she put something; in other, more dangerous cases, even a tiny nap could cause a severe car accident.[9]

Sleep doctor Neil Feldman, M.D., noted that narcolepsy can "severely compromise normal activities and quality of life." Embarrassment and falls may result from cataplectic attacks, when the narcoleptic is fully aware of his or her surroundings but cannot move. Feldman says, "Teenagers with narcolepsy can be viewed as poorly motivated or depressed, making school challenging or the work place a difficult and uncomfortable environment," and these situations could progress to causing low self-esteem, social isolation and shame. Symptoms of narcolepsy often occur during adolescence, but frequently the diagnosis is not made until sufferers reach adulthood.[10]

Two other frightening symptoms of narcolepsy involve sleep paralysis and hallucinations. In sleep paralysis, the person temporarily loses the ability to move or speak while falling asleep or waking up. When experiencing this symptom, many patients fear that they may be permanently paralyzed or even die; however, after the episode ends, people rapidly recover their full capacity to move and speak.[11]

Although no cure has yet been found for narcolepsy, medication or lifestyle changes can make a difference. Helpful lifestyle hints for narcoleptics, according to the National Institute of Neurological Disorders and Stroke, include

1. maintaining a regular sleep schedule
2. avoiding alcohol and caffeine-containing beverages for several hours before bedtime
3. avoiding smoking, especially at night
4. maintaining a comfortable, adequately warmed bedroom environment
5. engaging in relaxing activities such as a warm bath before bedtime.

Other tips include taking regularly scheduled naps during the day or exercising for at least 20 minutes per day at least 4 or 5 hours before bedtime.

When changing sleep habits is not enough to stop the symptoms, many different types of medications are available. Commonly prescribed drugs for narcolepsy are stimulants, antidepressants, and sodium oxybate. Stimulants, drugs that "speed up" the central nervous system, are often prescribed to help people with narcolepsy stay awake during the day. Amphetamines (such as Adderall or Dexedrine) or methylphenidates (such as Concerta or Ritalin) help to combat the daytime sleepiness. Care must be taken with amphetamines to avoid addiction or possible side effects, such as nervousness and heart pal-pitations. A newer drug, provigil (Modafinil), has been developed specifically for the daytime sleepiness of narcolepsy.[12]

Selective serotonin or norepinephrine reuptake inhibitors are another category of medication that curbs REM sleep to stop the symptoms of cataplexy, hallucinations, and sleep paralysis. Some drugs in this category are atomoxetine (Strattera), fluoxetine (Prozac and Sarafem), and venlafax-ine (Effexor). Side effects from these medications can range from digestive problems, jitteriness, and restlessness to headache and insomnia. Antidepres-sants, including protriptyline (Vivactil) and imipramine (Tofranil), are effec-tive for cataplexy, but may cause dry mouth and constipation, among other side effects.[13]

All medications have side effects, so nobody should take these drugs unless they are prescribed by a doctor.

SLEEP APNEA

At least 10 million Americans have another sleep disorder called sleep apnea, a treatable condition that causes a person to stop breathing during sleep.[14] This happens for about 10 seconds, in younger people the equiva-lent of about 2 and a half breaths. There are three main types of sleep apnea: obstructive, central, or mixed. During the most common apnea, obstruc-tive, the soft tissue in the back of the throat collapses and obstructs the air-way. This could happen as often as 100 times per night, and could last for a minute or longer. Because the brain still knows what is happening even during sleep, it sends a signal to wake up the person just enough to start breathing again. Most people do not even know that this is happening, but because of their interrupted sleep pattern, they are often sleepy during the day. As with other sleep conditions, side effects of sleep apnea, especially in younger people, include problems concentrating on the job or in school, and car accidents. The less common form of apnea, central sleep apnea, occurs when the brain fails to send the appropriate signals to the breathing muscles to initiate breathing.

Obesity is another cause of sleep apnea. According to the National Heart, Lung and Blood Institute, more than half of people with sleep apnea are overweight. The excess amount of tissue in the airway causes it to be narrowed so the air cannot easily flow into or out of the nose or mouth. This causes heavy snoring, periods of no breathing, and frequent changes from a heavy sleep to light sleep. Exercise and diet control resulting even in a few lost pounds can help in these cases.

Sleep apnea is especially dangerous when the sufferer also drinks or takes sleeping pills. This combination can increase the frequency and length of breathing pauses in people with sleep apnea.[15] Alcohol relaxes the throat muscles and affects the brain's breathing center. When mixed with alcohol, apnea can cause irregular heartbeat, stroke, and even death.

Treatment of sleep apnea requires long-term management, but seeking treatment is well worth the effort. When left untreated, sleep apnea can cause high blood pressure, heart attack, stroke, obesity, diabetes, and irregular heart-beat. Lifestyle changes, mouthpieces, surgery, and/or breathing devices have proven successful. Avoiding alcohol and medicines that cause drowsiness will

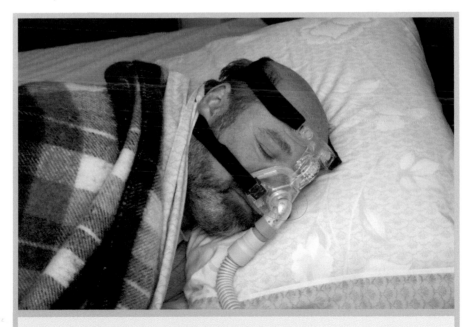

Figure 3.3 Sleep apnea causes a person to stop breathing during sleep. A common treatment is the continuous positive airway pressure (CPAP) machine, which gently blows air into the throat during sleep, pressing on the airway to keep it open. (© *Shutterstock*)

TO SLEEP, PERCHANCE TO DREAM—
WHY DREAMING IS IMPORTANT

In dreams, a person can be a flying superhero or trapped on an alien spaceship. Many have dreamed of missing final exams, or on the way to the important job interview, discover that they have forgotten their pants. Dreams range from the realistic to the absurd, from sweet dreams to nightmares. Scientists continue to research the causes of dreams and their meaning.

Since dreams take place in the mind, there is no definitive explanation of their meaning. Dreams may represent wants or fears or a way to work out problems; or they could be just a mix of situations and people we see in daily life, on TV, or in video games. In the case of recurring dreams, the mind may be singling out a certain fear or circumstance that needs particular attention or solution. Nightmares may make for some monstrous moments during the night. Nightmares usually occur during REM sleep, but night terrors happen before the REM phase, within the first hour or two of going to bed. Night terrors are frightening for the people having them and for those who watch them. During a night terror, the dreamer may sit up in bed screaming with her eyes wide open.

Some scientists believe that it is possible to stop nightmares and night terrors by concentrating very hard during waking hours or before sleeping to "change" the events or ending of the dream.[16] These thoughts, it is believed, may sink in and stop the nightmares.

make it easier for the throat to stay open during sleep. Losing weight or maintaining a healthy weight, sleeping on the side instead of the back, and quitting smoking all can help to keep the breathing passages open during the night. Some dentists can make mouthpieces to treat mild sleep apnea. The mouthpiece adjusts the lower jaw and tongue to keep the airways open.

A very common treatment for sleep apnea is the use of the CPAP (continuous positive airway pressure) machine, a device made up of a mask that fits over the mouth and nose, or just over the nose, that gently blows air into

Another method of changing the course of a dream is connected with a concept called **lucid dreaming**, during which a person realizes during the dream that he or she is dreaming and becomes empowered to control what happens in the dream. Dream researcher Stephen LaBerge, founder of the Lucidity Institute, asserts that developing lucid dreaming skills can promote personal development, enhance self-confidence, overcome nightmares, improve mental (and perhaps physical) health, and facilitate creative problem solving.[17] Lucid dreaming is difficult to achieve because it must occur during parts of the sleep cycle when the mind is in a less-deep dream stage.

Many circumstances affect the sleep cycle. Students are often sleep deprived because of staying up late cramming for exams, late parties, waking up early because of school or work schedules, difficulty sleeping due to stress, or environmental factors such as noise in the house or a busy neighborhood. After sleep testing, some physicians may find it necessary to establish a consistent sleep pattern with sleep medications. When used correctly, these drugs can be quite helpful. However, sleep medications do not just put a person to sleep—they override the body's natural sleep mechanisms, causing side effects when the medication wears off or is not continued. It is important to take sleep medications under the supervision of a doctor, and taking them improperly could constitute drug abuse. Taking sleep drugs to regulate sleep without a prescription or taking them improperly can create sleep disorders that were not present before the drugs were abused.

the throat, pressing on the airway and keeping it open. Another treatment is to undergo surgery to widen the breathing passages. This is done by removing excess tissue in the mouth or throat or resetting the lower jaw. Some people also have surgery to remove the tonsils if they are blocking the airway.[18]

Besides testing at a sleep center, some dental professionals such as orthodontists use X-rays to diagnose sleep apnea. After taking an X-ray, the dentist can determine the position of the tongue and the hyoid bone. If the bone sits low, the patient is more at risk for apnea.

RESTLESS LEGS SYNDROME

This syndrome may be annoying during the day, but during the night, it causes even more frustration. **Restless legs syndrome** (RLS) involves an irresistible urge to move the legs. During the day, students with RLS have problems sitting in the classroom. Feeling strange sensations in their legs like crawling, cramping, tugging, tingling, or burning, they move their legs to ease the discomfort. Jiggling legs can be distracting to the person, nearby students, and even the teacher. Some RLS sufferers even must get up and walk around, and then they may be tagged as "problem students." At night, perhaps because of the inactivity of lying in bed, the symptoms often get worse, causing a need to get up and walk around. Not only do people with RLS need more time to fall asleep because of this, but the urge to walk around to stop the feelings in the legs keeps the person in a wakeful state. Moving one's legs all night of course results in sleepiness the next day. That is why students with RLS frequently experience academic problems, irritability, moodiness, concentration problems, and what looks like hyperactivity.[19]

Diagnosis for RLS is made after checking the patient's history for other illnesses, and noting the symptoms. Sometimes, a sleep study may be ordered. RLS is treated with behavior changes and medications. Heating pads, cold compresses, or rubbing the legs can relieve some of the nighttime discomfort. Cutting out caffeine may help. Nutritionally, some people with RLS have low folic acid or iron levels, and can benefit from taking vitamin supplements.

Certain over-the-counter medications just make RLS worse. These products include drugs to treat nausea, colds, allergies, and depression. If lifestyle changes do not help enough to allow a good night's sleep, some physicians will prescribe medications to treat this condition. Some of these medications were developed for other conditions, but have positive effects when taken for RLS.

For people with moderate to severe RLS, doctors recommend drugs usually taken for **Parkinson's disease**, a disorder of the central nervous system characterized by shaking and impaired muscle coordination. These drugs reduce the amount of leg movement by affecting the level of the chemical messenger **dopamine** in the brain. Two drugs, ropinirole (Requip) and pramipexole (Mirapex), are approved by the Food and Drug Administration for the treatment of moderate to severe RLS. Certain medications for **epilepsy**, a central nervous system disorder characterized by loss of consciousness and seizures, such as gabapentin (Neurontin), may also relieve symptoms.[20]

Moderate to severe symptoms of RLS can also be treated with opioids such as codeine, oxycodone (Roxicodone), a combination of oxycodone and acetaminophen (Percocet, Roxicet), and the combination medicine hydrocodone and acetaminophen (Lortab, Vicodin).[21] Because these drugs are very dangerous and addictive, they are usually prescribed only as a last resort. They must be used with extreme caution, and only with monitoring by a physician.

Benzodiazepines relax muscles and cause sleep in people with RLS, but they do not change the discomfort of the leg sensations—they only make the person drowsy enough to fall asleep. They may cause daytime drowsiness. Commonly prescribed sedatives for RLS include clonazepam (Klonopin), triazolam (Halcion), eszopiclone (Lunesta), ramelteon (Rozerem), temazepam (Restoril), zaleplon (Sonata), and zolpidem (Ambien).

Another type of drug used for RLS are from a group called **alpha-2 agonists**, drugs that stimulate alpha-2 receptors in the brain stem, activating nerve cells that quiet the part of the nervous system that controls muscle movements and sensations. An example of this is clonidine (Catapres).[22] Receptors are structures on or inside of cells that receive certain substances. The **alpha-2 agonists** are drugs that stimulate these receptors in the brain stem, activating nerve cells that quiet this part of the nervous system.

Another disorder that causes leg movement during sleep, but for different reasons, is **periodic limb movement disorder** (PLMD), which is characterized by rhythmic leg movements during sleep. This differs from RLS because PLMD is not caused by strange sensations in the legs, and it occurs only during sleep. This disorder is not very common in younger people.

Diagnosis is important for these sleep disorders so that proper treatment can be started as soon as possible. Getting sleep patterns back on track will result in a happier person, better grades, and a safer night's sleep.

4
Sleep Drugs

For a high school senior, Keith's life seemed pretty normal. He was in the marching band, had a part-time job, got good grades, and was close to his family. He never got in trouble with the police and never even got pulled over for a ticket. That is why, when Keith got addicted to depressants, not many people noticed—until the day that his dog found him, floating in the backyard pool.

At the busiest time of the school year, Keith started to feel a lot of pressure. He visited the doctor and said that although he was trying his best to keep up with all of his activities, he felt agitated and worried most of the time, and had trouble falling asleep. The doctor prescribed a benzodiazepine drug, one that taken according to instructions would just "take the edge off" of the more stressful days. These helped ease his tension and let him feel like he was more in control of this life.

As the year progressed, and Keith attended parties, he would take his pill before having a few drinks. He had a great time at these parties—at least that is what the others told him, since he couldn't always remember what happened that night. Over time the dose that he needed to get the same effect increased. Keith worried that asking the doctor for more would raise suspicion; instead, it was easy enough to find a friend of a friend who could get him all of the sedatives that he wanted, although not always the same brand or the same strength. By this time, it didn't matter, because he just took whatever pills were available for sale at the time, although sedatives were his favorites.

Keith lost his job at the deli counter in the local supermarket even though his friends in the department tried to cover up for him. He had begun to arrive late after oversleeping, and he often carelessly left the freezer door open. Once he even accidentally cut himself. Finally the manager let him go, and told him that he needed to get some help for whatever was bothering him. Much of the time, though, Keith still went to school, and for the most part he seemed just like the guy he had always been, only more tired and more accident prone. His busy family ignored what was happening to Keith, believing it was part of the exhaustion of a busy teenage schedule. When his grades began to slip and his parents confronted him, Keith told them that he got too involved with his extracurricular activities and senior celebrations, and promised to try harder.

Almost a year after Keith started experimenting with sedatives, he knew something had to be done. He was having trouble concentrating, was spending a lot of money, and he had lost some friends that he valued. Sometimes he became agitated and argumentative, usually when taking too much of whatever sedative that he could obtain at the time. He tried to stop on his own, but felt an awful pain in his stomach. He couldn't sleep regularly, and when he did, he had nightmares.

On the day that the dog found him, Keith had taken several sedatives. He didn't know their names or even remember who he got them from. By this time, he just pulled a few out of a bag that he kept under his bed. He just took a handful, to get rid of the terrible anxiety that he felt about nothing in particular. He must have decided that it was a good idea to go swimming, but he doesn't remember. His parents told him that the dog was barking excitedly, and when they went to investigate, they found him floating in the pool. He had hit his head when he dove in fully dressed, damaging his spine. Keith spent a few weeks in the hospital to regain his brain function and also spent some time in a rehabilitation facility. Keith now speaks at high schools about getting addicted to depressants. The stresses of being in a wheelchair and starting college still make him crave and want to buy tranquilizers, but he says that he has already paid too high a price.

To start the sleep process at bedtime or maintain sleep throughout the night, the body goes through many chemical and physical processes. Sleep drugs help the body return to a healthy sleep pattern when circumstances have altered the natural rhythms of the night, and usually the results are positive. Taking the wrong dosage or mixing with other medications or alcohol can be life altering or life threatening. When used according to directions and under a doctor's care, sleep medications can help someone with a sleep disorder to achieve a restful night's sleep and to adjust the sleep cycle, so that ultimately, the body will be able to regulate itself.

OVER-THE-COUNTER SLEEP MEDICATIONS

Over-the-counter sleep medications have both good and bad aspects—they prevent sleepless nights, and they are readily available in the grocery, drug store, or even at gas station mini-marts. However, even though they can be purchased in the same place as a favorite energy drink or breakfast cereal, they still must be taken with caution.

The side effect of drowsiness caused by certain medications makes them attractive to people who have trouble falling asleep. For example, antihistamines relieve allergy symptoms by blocking the action of histamine, a chemical released by the immune system in allergic reactions. When the body is exposed to an allergen (any substance that can cause an allergy), it releases histamines that attach to the body's cells and cause them to swell and leak fluid, causing itching, sneezing, runny nose, and watery eyes. Antihistamines are categorized either as H1 blockers or H2 blockers, depending on the type of receptors on the cell surface that they act on. Antihistamines prevent the histamines from attaching to the cells.

Certain over-the-counter allergy medicines that contain antihistamines cause drowsiness. One of the most common antihistamines is diphenhydramine, an ingredient in the well-known drug Benadryl. Diphenhydramine is also found in drugs designed specifically for sleep, such as Nytol, Sleep-Eez, and Sominex. Sometimes, this ingredient is paired with pain relievers, resulting in the "P.M." medications, such as Tylenol PM and Excedrin PM. Other antihistamines will tackle cold, flu, and allergy symptoms and also promise a good night's sleep, like the chlorpheniramine in Chlor-Trimeton,

Figure 4.1 Nytol, an over-the-counter sleep drug containing diphenhydramine, is a sedating histamine. (*© Photo Researchers*)

hydroxyzine in Atarax or Vistaril, and the doxylamine in Vicks NyQuil and Alka-Seltzer Plus Night-Time Cold Medicine. First-generation antihistamines also work in the part of the brain that controls nausea and vomiting, so they can also be used to help prevent motion sickness. Because one of the most common side effects of first-generation antihistamines is sleepiness, they are popular with people who have trouble sleeping (insomnia). While these drugs may cause the sleep that is desired, most of them could also cause next-day drowsiness, dizziness, drunken movements, blurred vision, or dry mouth and throat.

Newer antihistamines, referred to as "second generation," were formulated to cause less drowsiness. Examples of this are loratadine, contained in Alavert and Claritin, and cetirizine in Zyrtec.[1] Second-generation antihistamines are not intended to cause sleepiness because they do not cross the **blood-brain barrier**, the protective network of blood vessels and cells that filters blood flowing to the brain.

CENTRAL NERVOUS SYSTEM

The body is a complicated mix of organs, tissues, muscles, nerves, and other parts that work together to help a person walk, talk, think, eat, and sleep. Each body part plays an important role in the body, but the brain, is, well, the brains of the operation. It controls thinking, feeling, learning, memory movement, and the operation of many of the organs such as the heart and the digestive system. When the brain needs to communicate with the rest of the body, the central nervous system relays messages to all the other systems in the body. The messages are sent through the spinal cord, which runs from the brain down the back. Along the cord, threadlike nerves branch out to every organ and body part. For example, if someone's hand touches a hot surface, the nerves in the hand send a message to the spinal cord and then to the brain telling it that something painful is happening. After receiving that message, the brain acknowledges the muscles' reflex action of pulling the hand off of the hot surface. Thankfully, this complicated exchange of information happens in a matter of seconds to protect the body from discomfort and harm.

CNS DEPRESSANTS

Many sleep medications work by targeting the central nervous system (CNS). Barbiturates slow down the activity of nerves, muscles, heart tissue, and the brain. As sedative-hypnotics, barbiturates' action on the central nervous system can range from mild sedation to coma and even death, depending on the dosage. Besides drowsiness, these medications can cause behavior similar to drunkenness, lack of muscle coordination, depression, and addiction. When mixed with alcohol, the combination can be fatal. Because of these dangers, barbiturates have lost popularity, and have been replaced by safer sedative-hypnotics, the benzodiazepines. This type of medication is also known to be **anxiolytic**, or anxiety reducing; however, they are also addictive, and in some cases, have become subject to abuse. Within this category, are mephobarbital (Mebaral), secobarbital (Seconal) and pentobarbital sodium (Nembutal).

Benzodiazepines affect the brain chemical **gamma-aminobutyric acid** (GABA), which decreases brain activity. GABA is a **neurotransmitter**, an agent that transmits messages from one brain cell (neuron) to another and causes calming effects. Approximately 40% of the millions of neurons all over the brain respond to GABA's quieting influence. Taking benzodiazepines increases the natural action of GABA.[2]

When benzodiazepines increase GABA activity, the body experiences a calming effect. At first, CNS depressants can cause sleepiness and lack of coordination, but, when taken over a long time period, the body gets used to the drug and the effects begin to disappear. As a result, larger doses will be needed to achieve the same effect, as **tolerance** builds. Long-term use of this type of drug can lead to addiction. Among others, these benzodiazepines are prescribed for short-term treatment of sleep disorders: diazepam (Valium), triazolam (Halcion), alprazolam (Xanax), and estazolam (ProSom). Since this medication slows brain activity, when the person stops taking it after a long-term dependence, it could lead to **rebound**, when symptoms return more severely than before taking the drug. In extreme cases, the person can even experience seizures.[3] Drugs of this type show a growing popularity among teens. In 2007 a Monitoring the Future Study done by the University of Michigan showed that 6% of high school seniors reported abusing depressants, including Valium and Xanax, compared to 4% in 1995.[4]

Benzodiazepines are not selective in the receptor sites that they target in the brain—they target the areas that need to be shut down for sleep, but also the areas that people need when they are awake. Another type of CNS depressant, the non-benzodiazepines or sedative-hypnotics, is similar, but not the same. They are more selective in the brain cells that they target. In the short term, they allow a person to get enough rest to regain a healthy natural sleep schedule, but they should not be used over a long time period.

Sleep medications in this category such as zolpidem (Ambien), zaleplon (Sonata), and eszopiclone (Lunesta), are now commonly prescribed to treat sleep disorders. Although benzodiazepines work similarly to non-benzodiazepines, they are significantly different. Non-benzodiazepines have a relatively short half-life, which means that not as much of them builds up in the body. As a result, the person may not feel as groggy in the morning. The non-benzodiazepines also do not affect the stages of sleep as much as

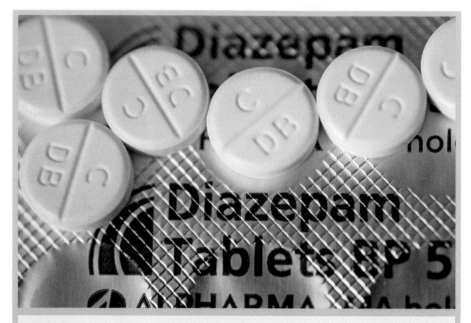

Figure 4.2 Diazepam (Valium) belongs to the sleep drug class known as benzodiazepines. (© *Alamy*)

the older medications, so the body does not feel more tired during the day because of the sleep cycle interruptions.

Each of the non-benzodiazepines has its own characteristics. Since zolpidem is long lasting, people should plan on getting at least 7–8 hours of sleep when they take it. It is not recommended to take it on the way home from a party, expecting to get to bed immediately after arriving home, because if the effects kick in sooner, the person could fall asleep at the wheel, become dizzy or disoriented. Zaleplon is the shortest-acting hypnotic available, meaning that it is rapidly eliminated from the body. Therefore, it is best for people who have difficulty falling asleep, but not those who wake up often throughout the night. Eszopiclone, a sleep medication that is approved for long-term use, may help improve both sleep maintenance and daytime alertness.

Ramelteon (Rozerem) is a sedative-hypnotic for people who have difficulty falling asleep, but it is not technically a non-benzodiazepine hypnotic. Unlike others that target GABA receptors, Ramelteon targets melatonin receptors, so it works similarly to the melatonin in the body. Ramelteon is not habit forming and is the first sleep drug not designated as a controlled substance,[5] but it should not be taken by someone also taking the antidepressant fluvoxamine (Luvox).

Non-benzodiazepine drugs can cause sleep-related behaviors such as driving, making phone calls, and preparing and eating food while asleep. Some stories of the side effects may sound funny, but could lead to serious consequences. According to a *Wall Street Journal* article, after taking non-benzodiazepine medications, "One woman woke up with a paintbrush in her hand, having painted her front door in her sleep. People have set fire to their kitchens while trying to cook, cursed their bosses on the phone and crashed their cars into trees—all in a sleeping pill-induced haze and with no memory afterward."[6]

This can occur even when taking the drug as directed by a doctor, but many cases of sleepwalking and sleep-driving have occurred when patients take these medications along with alcohol or other drugs or take more than the recommended dose. A severe allergic reaction (anaphylaxis) is facial swelling (angioedema) that can occur as early as the first time one of these drugs is taken.

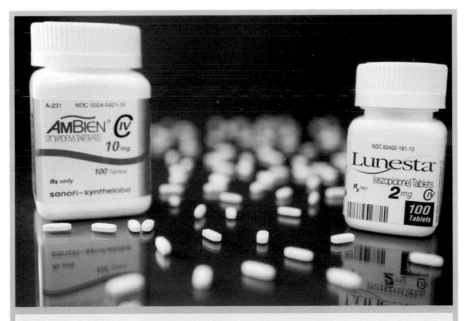

Figure 4.3 Zolpidem (Ambien) and eszopiclone (Lunesta) belong to the sleep drug class known as sedative-hypnotics or non-benzodiazepines. (© *Getty*)

HOW THE FOOD AND DRUG ADMINISTRATION ENSURES DRUG SAFETY

Before a drug is offered for sale in a pharmacy or over the counter, it must first undergo testing to discover possible side effects and safety. The U.S. Food and Drug Administration (FDA) evaluates every facet of the drug, including manufacturing conditions, the manufacturer's design of clinical trials, and all of the possible side effects. Below are some of the steps to bringing a new drug to market.

Researchers or companies developing a drug must show the FDA results of preclinical testing in laboratory animals, and then propose their plan for clinical trials (human testing). Before clinical trials, the company must define the type of people who will participate in the study, the tests, medicines and dosages, the length of the study, and objectives. Testing participants must be fully informed of their risks, and researchers must take appropriate steps to protect patients from harm.

Three phases of clinical trials follow. Phase one shows safety issues, such as side effects and how the medicine works inside the body and how it gets out. Phase two focuses on effectiveness, and Phase three expands on both of the earlier studies, adding different types of people, different dosages, and using the drug in combination

Anyone who receives a prescription for these medicines will also get a patient medication guide explaining the risks of the drugs and the precautions to take. Ask the prescribing doctor any questions concerning these drugs or their potential side effects.

CNS STIMULANTS

CNS depressants get the body to sleep. CNS stimulants do just the opposite. For people suffering from narcolepsy, who can fall asleep while driving, at school, or at work, these drugs can help them to live a more normal life.

with other drugs. Participants in clinical trials can range from a few hundred to about 3,000 people, and the trials can take several years.

After the clinical trials there is much work still to be done. A New Drug Application (NDA) comprises all of the information gained from the preclinical and clinical trials, as well as manufacturing information. For 6 to 10 months an FDA review team—medical doctors, chemists, statisticians, microbiologists, pharmacologists, and other experts—explores the studies for safety and effectiveness. Since all drugs have side effects, the definition of *safe* is when the benefits of the drug appear to outweigh the risks.

After all the testing, the FDA reviews information for the instructions and labeling and inspects the manufacturing facilities. Even all this testing cannot discover all potential problems with a drug, so the FDA continues to track approved drugs for problems or issues through a post-marketing surveillance program.

The FDA takes all these steps to protect the public. After all that work, it is up to the person taking the medication to follow the instructions responsibly. To find out if a drug has been approved by the FDA, check out Drugs@FDA, a list of FDA-approved drug products and drug labeling.

Source: U.S. Food and Drug Administration, "The FDA's Drug Review Process: Ensuring Drugs Are Safe and Effective," http://www.fda.gov/drugs/resourcesforyou/consumers/ucm143534.htm (accessed January 19, 2011).

Stimulants affect levels of chemicals in the brain that increase blood pressure and heart rate, constrict blood vessels, increase blood glucose, and stimulate the respiratory system. These drugs can cause irregular heartbeat and increase potential for seizures, and they should not be taken along with antidepressants or over-the-counter cold medications that contain decongestants because of the potential for problems with the blood pressure or heart.

Medications used to control attention deficit disorders can also help teenagers feel more alert and focused. A survey by the Partnership for a Drug-Free America shows that 1 in 10 teenagers has used the stimulants Ritalin or Adderall for nonmedical purposes.[7] The U.S. Department of Justice voiced concern about the widespread use of such attention-deficit drugs. Its report said, "Methylphenidate is routinely portrayed as a benign, mild substance that is not associated with abuse or serious side effects. In reality, however, the scientific literature indicates that methylphenidate shares the same abuse potential as other Schedule II stimulants. Further, case reports document that methylphenidate abuse can lead to tolerance and severe psychological dependence."[8]

OPIOIDS

Opioids are designated as **analgesic**, or pain-relieving, medications. This type of drug acts by attaching to specific proteins called opioid receptors, which are found in the brain, spinal cord, and gastrointestinal tract, thereby changing the way a person experiences pain. Although drowsiness is one of the many side effects of opioids, they also depress breathing, which could cause serious results when taken by someone with sleep apnea. In fact, opioid-based pain medications may cause sleep apnea, according to an article in *Pain Medicine*, the journal of the American Academy of Pain Medicine.[9]

Although opioids are taken orally as prescribed by doctors, in situations of drug abuse, pills have also been crushed and the powder snorted or injected. Many deaths have resulted from unprescribed use of these types of opiates. Snorting or injecting opioids causes a rapid release of the drug into the bloodstream, and drugs like oxycodone (OxyContin) are designed in slow-release formulations. Crushing the pill introduces it into the body in high doses, increasing the possibility of an overdose.

These medications are safe to use with other substances only under a physician's supervision. They should not be used with alcohol, antihistamines, barbiturates, or benzodiazepines. Because these other substances slow breathing, their effects in combination with opioids could lead to life-threatening respiratory depression.

Patients who are prescribed opioids for a period of time may develop a physical dependence, increasing tolerance, and even withdrawal symptoms when stopping use. Therefore, people taking prescribed opioid medications should be under appropriate medical supervision while taking them and also when stopping to reduce or avoid withdrawal symptoms. After opioid use, withdrawal symptoms such as restlessness, muscle and bone pain, insomnia, diarrhea, and vomiting can hinder sleep.[10]

SLEEP SUPPLEMENTS

Even "natural" or herbally derived sleep-inducing medications and supplements must be chosen for specific needs. They may seem harmless, but they should still be chosen cautiously because of possible interactions with prescription medications. Also, since many companies that manufacture herbal supplements are not required to have approval from the FDA, some companies may not produce their products under healthy or safe processes, or pursue research on how well the product works. Also, many companies are not required to standardize manufacturing processes, so the effectiveness or

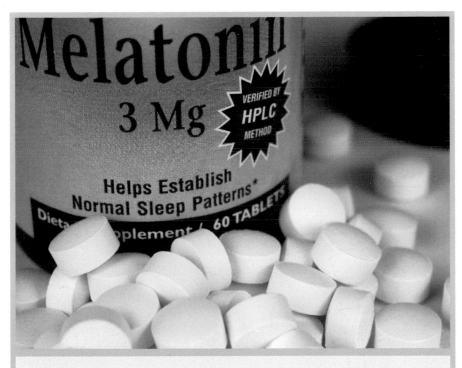

Figure 4.4   Although melatonin plays a role in the body's ability to fall asleep and stay asleep, effective supplement dosages have not been established. (© *Photo Researchers*)

side effects of their products may differ among brands or even within different lots of the same brand. Some dietary supplements that are considered for sleep difficulties are melatonin, valerian root, and kava. Although melatonin plays a role in the body's ability to fall asleep and stay asleep, effective dosages still have not been established. When taken in too large amounts, it may cause sleeplessness, headaches, nightmares, and mental impairment. Proper dosage, when determined by a medical professional, can help with jet lag and delayed sleep syndrome.

Dietary supplements made from valerian root and kava have also been marketed as sleep aids. Valerian has sedative qualities, but not enough tests have been conducted to show it to be effective. The supplement is made from the roots and stems of the valerian plant, processed into tea form or capsules. Few side effects have been reported, but they do include mild headache or stomach upset, abnormal heartbeat, and insomnia. Very bad effects have been reported from kava. The National Center for Complementary and Alternative Medicine (NCCAM) cautions that this herb has been reported to cause liver damage, including hepatitis and liver failure (which can cause death), as well as abnormal muscle spasm or involuntary muscle movements. Over the long term, kava may result in scaly, yellowed skin. Even though this is an herbal supplement, NCCAM warns against driving and operating heavy machinery while taking kava because of its possibility of causing drowsiness. Kava interacts poorly with medications such as alprazolam, used for anxiety, and it has also been shown to increase the strength of other sleep medications, alcohol, and antidepressants.[11]

5

Diagnosing Sleep Disorders

Sherise is a very busy teenager. She belongs to an honor society, Spanish Club, a theater group, and works on the yearbook. She needs her after-school job at the coffee shop to pay her car insurance and fund her shoe addiction. She leaves her house early in the morning, before 7 A.M., to get to school, and on most days arrives home about an hour before she has to go to bed. On the weekend, she divides her time among her family, her boyfriend, work, and study, and keeps in touch with her family and friends by cell phone, calling and texting to check in.

By the time she arrived home each night, Sherise was tired, but still had some work to do. She drank an energy drink just to get the second wind that she needed to finish homework and finish the day. Several hours later, when she got into bed, her mind was still racing with assignments that needed to be done the next day and things she needed to tell her boyfriend and friends. Often, just when she was about to fall asleep, her cell phone would ring, that familiar rhythm that told her that she just received a text. She would get up to check what it was and then return to bed. Plugged in right next to her bed, her phone usually woke her up several times during the night.

During the next few months, Sherise found that she was falling asleep later and later, because of her workload and waiting for the last of her evening calls. One night she was exhausted, but her mind was racing too fast for her to fall asleep. She checked the medicine cabinet in her parents' bathroom and found a bottle of Xanax that her mother had recently been prescribed to reduce her anxiety. Sherise thought that it would calm her down enough to go to sleep. It worked well, but she found that by the middle of the night, when the phone woke her up, she needed another pill to get back to sleep. After using up all the pills in the prescription bottle, Sherise found a friend at school who knew someone who could get her more pills. Apparently her parents never noticed their prescriptions disappearing.

During the next few months, Sherise began to get jittery during the day, so she took an extra pill at school to calm her nerves. She started to get nervous about being addicted, so one night she planned not to take any pills. She developed a pounding headache and the feeling of being disconnected from her surroundings, so she gave in and started taking pills again. At this point, desperate to sleep, she took any pills that her friend at school could get her. Even with the pills eventually making her sleep, she was exhausted the next day. Her grades started slipping, and so did her driving skills. When she backed into her father's car in the driveway one morning, it made her parents take a closer look at what was happening.

Sherise told her parents about the pills that she was taking. She didn't know what she was taking; all she knew was that they were supposed to get her to sleep. All three of them went to a doctor who worked with Sherise to slowly wean her off the drugs. He substituted other drugs to counteract the side effects that kept her stomach in knots and her mind unable to organize her thoughts properly.

It took a long time and a lot of willpower before her cravings reduced. She still wanted those drugs at times, but knew that she had worked hard to function without them. Then the doctor referred her to a sleep clinic. After testing, the sleep doctor found that she suffered from delayed sleep phase syndrome, partially due to her age and hectic schedule. She was reluctant to start with sleep medications again, but agreed to a small dose of melatonin to start the process. Sherise worked out a sleep schedule with her doctor that was designed to get her to bed at a time that was right for her body clock. It is starting to work, and Sherise is optimistic that her new schedule will help her achieve the goals that she has always dreamed of.

Sleep disorders are common in teens but often are not recognized. According to the Cleveland Clinic, sleep disturbances in some form are seen in as many as 30% of children, and biological-clock delays can be se[e] of teens.[1]

SLEEP DIARY

If someone consults a sleep specialist, it may be helpful to keep a sleep diary for one to two weeks so that there is a record of the amount and quality of sleep. A sleep diary provides insight into a person's nightly sleep patterns and tracks details that otherwise would be overlooked or forgotten. For example, reading before sleep can be a good way to get the mind off everyday occurrences and relax, but for others an exciting mystery or frightening thriller can stimulate both the mind and body. Some important night-details include the following:

1. When sleep is started, stopped, or interrupted
2. Occurrences before or during sleep that disrupt sleep
3. Usual bedtime
4. How long it takes to fall asleep after getting into bed
5. The lighting in the room
6. Time of any disruptions
7. Number of awakenings during the night
8. Number and type of dreams
9. Morning awakenings, specifically what time and how long after awakening the person gets out of bed
10. How the person feels in the morning (energetic, still tired, exhausted, and so on).

If someone else is in the room, it is also helpful for him or her to record the person's behavior while sleeping. Snoring, tossing and turning, and talking or yelling while sleeping are all clues to what is happening during specific times of the night. Before trying to fall asleep, the diary-keeper should also list actions that may affect the sleep process. The list should include beverages, meals or snacks before bed, exercise schedule, medications, times and duration of naps, and times of smoking and drinking alcohol or caffeinated drinks. It is important to list all types of medications and drugs. In order to unlock the mystery of sleep, the doctor needs all of the pieces of the puzzle.

SLEEPINESS QUESTIONNAIRE

The **Epworth Sleepiness Scale** is another assessment for determining whether a sleep disorder is present. This eight-question assessment of day-time sleepiness asks how likely a person is to fall asleep in a variety of situations, ranging from talking to a friend to waiting at a red light. Scores less than 10 are considered normal, and those higher than 10 indicate a need for additional evaluation by a sleep specialist.

After going to a general physician for a physical exam to rule out any possible illnesses that could cause sleep problems, the patient can ask for a recommendation to a sleep center to determine the sleep disorder and appropriate treatment. At the sleep center, the sleep doctor will evaluate the sleep diary and the Epworth Sleepiness Scale information provided by the patient, and will ask questions about the person's day and nighttime schedules, social life, eating, drinking and smoking habits, and other issues that affect sleep.

If an overnight study is needed, the person will be asked to go to a sleep center for testing. The sleep center has rooms equipped just like a bedroom to encourage relaxation and sleep. The patient arrives at the center in the evening. There is no need to worry about roommates or other people in the room because the tester wants to measure only the patient's physical responses during sleep. These responses can show whether the person has sleep apnea, restless legs syndrome, insomnia, sleep walking, night terrors, or narcolepsy. The technician or doctor will help set up the necessary equipment for the test. The patient is allowed to watch television or read to relax, and then it's lights out—time to go to sleep. When the patient goes to sleep, all the action starts in the sleep-monitoring area. A low-light video camera allows a sleep technician to watch the person from another room. The technician will enter the sleep room to adjust a sensor or detach wires for a bathroom visit.

To make the night as comfortable as possible, sleep centers usually advise people to eat normally and take necessary medications before reporting for the study. No over-the-counter sleep medications should be taken for three days before the study, and no naps the day of the study. To help the electrodes to stick to the scalp better, people should shampoo their hair on the day of the test and not use any hair products, even conditioner. Patients should bring pajamas, a favorite pillow, a bedtime snack, reading material, toothbrush, and toothpaste.

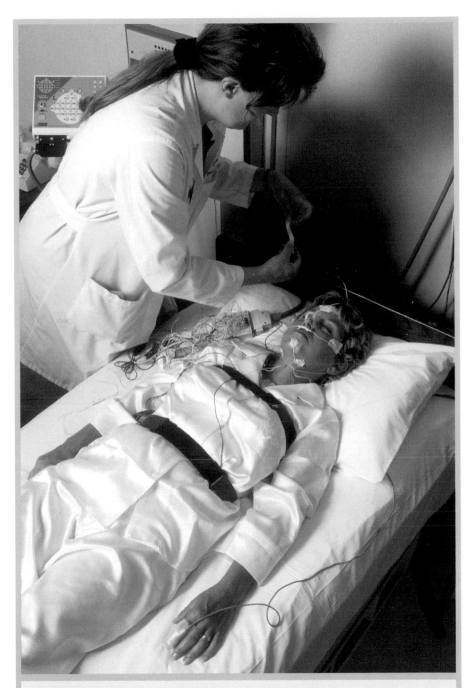

Figure 5.1 A patient is prepared for a sleep study at a sleep center lab. (© *Photo Researchers*)

SLEEP TIPS FOR TEENS

- **Maximize sleep time.** While studies have shown that teens need about 9 hours of sleep to feel rested, that is not a realistic goal for many. A person should try to keep a similar sleep schedule each day and, if the schedule must be varied, keep the change within one hour.
- **Exercise.** Thirty to 60 minutes four times a week is suggested for a healthier body and mind. But exercising within two to three hours of bedtime can result in difficulty falling asleep.
- **Eat something.** It is difficult to go to sleep hungry. A small snack eaten near bedtime, such as a glass of milk, some fruit, cereal, or crackers, may help. Fatty foods and heavy meals should be avoided within 1 to 2 hours of sleeping.
- **Cut the caffeine.** Coffee, iced tea, colas, energy drinks, and chocolate are stimulating foods that can delay sleep.
- **Take a daytime nap.** There are varying opinions about whether teens should take naps during the day. If a nap is needed, it should be limited to 20 to 30 minutes in the early afternoon. Napping too close to bedtime can give the body a "second wind" and prevent sleeping during the night.

POLYSOMNOGRAM

When testing for excessive daytime sleepiness, insomnia, sleep apnea, or narcolepsy, a **polysomnogram**—a diagnostic sleep study—is taken to evaluate the body's various activities during sleep. Before bedtime, a technologist places electrodes on the patient's head, face, chest, and legs. Elastic bands are placed around the chest and stomach to measure breathing movements. These are connected to a computer. Wires attached to the electrodes are long enough for the person to move around and turn over in bed. A polysomnogram measures brain waves, heartbeat, breathing, eye and leg movements, and muscle tension during sleep. This test measures the details of sleep, such as how long

- **Turn off the phone.** The phone should be turned off when starting bedtime rituals.
- **Avoid alcohol or smoking.** Besides just being healthier, this is especially important when trying to sleep. Cigarettes contain nicotine, which is a stimulant. Smokers should not indulge within an hour of bedtime. Alcohol also should not be used before bed because it disrupts the REM stage of sleep.
- **Calm down.** A relaxing activity before bedtime, such as reading or listening to soft music, may help sleep. Loud or fast-paced music and books that have exciting plots should be avoided.
- **Bed = Sleep.** The bed should be used for sleeping only. This trains the body to think that when it hits the soft mattress, it should know that sleep is the next logical step.
- **Create atmosphere.** Unnecessary distractions should be avoided. Lights should be dim or off. Demanding reading can be removed from the bedstand, and computers can be put away.
- **Shhhhhh.** Light sleepers can try using a fan or a "white noise" machine that makes a constant low sound to drown out all of the other interesting nightly house noises.

it takes to fall asleep, how long it takes to enter the REM part of the sleep cycle, and changes in breathing and heart rate. Some people either stop breathing or almost stop breathing during the night, and do not even know it, so this is a good opportunity to find out how many times that happens. Although people probably will not sleep as well as at home, they do fall asleep enough for the technician to get important information. In the morning, the technician removes the sensors and the test is over.

The sleep doctor will evaluate the test by looking for certain evidence of sleeping disorders. For example, if breathing stops completely for 10 seconds, that is indicative of a type of apnea. **Hypoapnea** is when the breathing is partially blocked for 10 seconds. If this happens 5 to 15 times per night the apnea is mild. Fifteen to 30 times per night mean the apnea is moderate and more than 30 times per night means it is severe.[2]

To assess sleep patterns for a longer period of time, sleep researchers use an **actigraph**, a small, wristwatch-like device that is applied at the sleep center and then worn for seven days afterward. The actigraph has an **accelerometer**, a type of meter that records movement, and also a light sensor and event-marker button. The light sensor keeps track of when lights are turned on and off. The event-marker button can be pushed to show when the patient went to bed or awoke. It is waterproof, so it does not have to be removed for the whole week, even in the shower.[3] This information is helpful because it records sleep when the person is in his or her own bed and on a normal daily schedule. After the seven days, the actigraph is returned to the sleep center and the information is downloaded into the computer and printed so that the activity can be reviewed.

To determine certain nighttime breathing disorders, **pulse oximetry** uses selected wavelengths of light to determine the oxygen saturation in the blood. A machine will be sent home with the person to use overnight and return to the sleep lab the next day. The machine has a clip that attaches over the end of the finger. A red light in the oximeter shines through the finger and measures the heart rate and oxygen content of the blood. Blood that contains a lot of oxygen is red, and blood that is poor in oxygen has more of a blue tone. Abnormal drops in the oxygen rate, or **desaturations**, may indicate sleep apnea because periodic pauses in the breathing are indicated by the drop in the blood oxygen level. The information is downloaded into a computer, and a report is generated for the physician to interpret.

After evaluating the results of all the sleep studies, the sleep doctor will meet with the patient to determine the best course of action for the specific sleep disorder that was discovered. In certain cases, sleep medications may be prescribed. Weight loss may be recommended to treat apnea, and a CPAP machine may be advised to help the sufferer breathe more easily at night.

6

Sleep Drug Abuse

When Brianna was invited to the party at a friend-of-a-friend's house, she was relieved that she had finally broken into a group at her new school. She was usually shy and thought it would be a good chance to make some new friends, so she decided to make an appearance. Besides, maybe she would find someone that she knew to hang out with.

With no parents in the house, alcohol flowed. On the dining room table, a punch bowl was filled with colorful pills that looked like candies. As more people arrived, she watched as they deposited pills from their pockets and purses. People would pass by and take a few from the bowl, washing the pills down with whatever was in their red plastic cups.

As she scanned the house for people that she knew, she noticed that some were dancing, others were talking, and some looked like they were sleeping on the couch. She headed toward the crowd, and after a while a guy came up to her and started a conversation. He seemed a bit drunk, but not too much, and they chatted about music. He seemed interested. He asked if he could get her a beer and, not wanting to seem uncool, she said yes. She figured that she could just sip it until she could put it down on a table somewhere.

After he brought her the beer, they continued talking. About 15 minutes later, Brianna started to feel unsteady. She thought it was the effect of the beer since she was not much of a drinker. She focused on a family portrait on the wall, and thought it was strange that the people in the portrait started to talk to her and move their arms, motioning for her to come closer. She felt nauseous, and couldn't really move very well. The guy started kissing her, and some girls who knew her from school told her afterward that she was all over him too.

That's all Brianna remembers. She ended up in the hospital that night. Test results showed that her drink was spiked with a depressant called flunitrazepam, better known by its nickname, roofies. Brianna had her first sexual experience that night, although she did not remember the incident or even who the guy was. She didn't remember throwing up all over the girls who tried to revive her after she passed out. It took about a week before she felt physically better, and she was very embarrassed about some of her actions at the party that she heard about later. During the next few weeks, she went to counseling to deal with her depression and anger. She still goes to parties, but only drinks from bottles or cans that she opens herself. She is still angry at the guy who gave her the drink, but she wouldn't even remember him if she saw him again, and he probably wouldn't remember her.

The perception about prescription medications is that since they are controlled and selectively doled out by doctors, they are safer from abuse. Unfortunately, this is not always true. While parents fear the influence of the local high school drug pusher, in fact, some very dangerous drugs are obtained through the doctors themselves or the parents' own medicine cabinet. According to data from the National Center on Addiction and Substance Abuse at Columbia University, a 2004 survey of physicians found that 43% did not ask about prescription-drug abuse when taking a patient's history, and one-third did not regularly call or obtain records from the patient's previous physician before prescribing potentially addictive drugs. Teens who are trying to obtain certain types of drugs know what symptoms to describe and what drugs treat those conditions. After listening to some teenagers' accounts of stress and sleep deprivation caused by overwork and pressure, well-meaning doctors too often respond with a prescription for controlled medications. Psychiatrist Richard A. Friedman wrote, "Claire, an 18-year-old who lives in Maine, told me, 'You can always find a doctor who you can convince that you have a sleeping problem to get Ambien [zolpidem] or that you have ADD [attention-deficit/hyperactivity disorder] and get Adderall.'" He noted that teenagers draw key distinctions between street drugs and prescription drugs, and self-medicate for "practical" purposes, such as using hypnotic drugs for sleep, stimulants to enhance their school performance, and tranquilizers such as benzodiazepines to decrease stress. Because the drugs are offered by a doctor, even if they are not directly prescribed, the teens perceive prescription drugs as "responsible," "controlled," or "safe."[1]

Besides directly getting the drugs from a doctor, some teens "share" prescriptions. In 2008 and 2009, more than half of the nonmedical users of prescription-type pain relievers, tranquilizers, stimulants, and sedatives used by adolescents aged 12 or older got the prescription drugs they used most recently "from a friend or relative for free." The majority indicated that their friend or relative had obtained the drugs from one doctor.[2]

Prescription drugs for sleep disorders are formulated to treat the symptoms that occur specifically because of that condition. These drugs have different effects depending upon the sleep disorder and the individual's needs for sleep and physical condition. Since these medications have the potential for dangerous side effects, doctors weigh potential benefits and risks for the individual patient.

WHAT IS THE RIGHT DOSE?

Before prescribing medication, the doctor considers the patient's weight and other medications. Each pill is manufactured to dissolve in the stomach at a certain time, to release drugs to the bloodstream at a certain rate, and to reach the brain in a certain way. When abused, taken in increased doses, mixed with other medicines or alcohol, or changed in form by crushing it, a drug may have the opposite effect than originally intended. For example, if a time-released pill that should be taken by mouth is crushed or inhaled, a 12-hour dose that was supposed to be slowly released over time can reach the central nervous system all at once, causing a deadly reaction.

WHAT ARE THE SIDE EFFECTS?

Even when used for an actual medical condition, drugs have side effects. For example, a stimulant such as Adderall increases attention span for school-work, but is also raises blood pressure and heart rate. On the other hand, a benzodiazepine can slow breathing. When combined with alcohol, which also slows breathing, the mixture can stop breathing altogether.

IS THE MEDICATION ADDICTING?

Medications that are taken properly and in prescribed doses are meant to balance out a physical, mental, or emotional problem so the person can act and react normally. Drugs that are abused are taken in the wrong dose by people whose bodies function normally without the drug. Even though the body does not need them, these medications still change the way the brain functions, and in higher doses than recommended. After drugs make the body feel good, they can make body feel bad. After a certain time, depending upon the chemicals involved, the drug alters the body's system, and it starts to crave the drug that made it feel good. Soon it becomes impossible to feel good without the drug in the system.

WHY DOES IT FEEL SO BAD WHEN THEY ARE STOPPED?

Since taking drugs changes the way the body and brain function, eventually the body adapts to the drug's presence, and when it is stopped, the person goes through withdrawal. Even when a person takes a medication exactly as prescribed by a doctor, suddenly stopping can cause very bad reactions. Withdrawal can cause nausea, chills, vomiting, muscle pain, and diarrhea. Symptoms that can often be controlled or reduced under a doctor's supervision.[3]

Depending upon how long the person has been taking the drug, withdrawal symptoms from sedative-hypnotics can include weakness, sweating, rapid pulse, tremors, or shaking, inability to sleep, nausea, vomiting, hallucinations, restlessness, anxiety, and irritability that can last for a few weeks. Stopping the drug suddenly could also result in seizures, coma, and death. It is important to go through withdrawal under the care of a doctor or drug rehabilitation program to provide a safe environment. In some cases, it is necessary to reduce the dose gradually, or substitute another, less harmful drug during the withdrawal process.

ON THE PHARM

Since socializing is an important part of teens' lives, drug abuse is often a part of the social scene. Many drugs have familiar "street names." Barbituates are called barbs, reds, red birds, phennies, tooies, yellows, or yellow jackets. Benzodiazpeines are called candy, downers, sleeping pills, or tranks. Individually, Ritalin is known as R-ball, Skippy, the smart drug, and vitamin R, and Rohypnol as the forget-me pill, Mexican Valium, R2, Roche, roofies, roofinol, rope, or rophies.[4]

While it is dangerous enough to take nonprescribed medications, more potential for harm exists in mixing medications only identified by their color and shape. "Pharm" parties (derived from the word *pharmaceutical*), make obtaining and taking pharmaceuticals into a dangerous guessing game. At these parties, each person attending brings some sort of pills. Many teens get the drugs from their own home medicine cabinet. Parents may be taking Xanax to reduce anxiety; they may not even take it anymore, and just be keeping it for an emergency. Another child in the family could be taking Ritalin for attention-deficit/hyperactivity disorder or painkillers after losing their wisdom teeth or breaking a bone. When the medicine cabinet is not locked up or checked, these storage spaces become prime places for drug shopping. Others get the drugs from Internet websites that do not require prescriptions. Each person at the party brings a handful of pills, and deposits them in a bowl. (The parties are sometimes also called "bowling" parties because of this.) Without knowing dose, side effects, or even what each pill is called, each teen takes a handful, sometimes washing it all down with alcohol. Sleep drugs, stimulants, antidepressants, painkillers, and many other categories all mixed together can cause hallucinations, euphoria, a feeling of great happiness and well-being, depression, and a range of other emotions. The interactions between the pills and the body's various very controlled and delicate chemically balanced systems often result in a trip to the emergency room, or in the worst case, the morgue.

Another potential for danger easily occurs at **raves**, high energy, all-night dance parties and clubs that feature dance music with a fast, pounding beat and choreographed laser programs.[5] A popular and dangerous drug that belongs to the benzodiazepine category is flunitrazepam (Rohypnol), commonly known as "roofies." Taken orally in a pill form or crushed and mixed

HELPING QUITTERS WIN

People with addictions to medications may need some encouragement to stop. Here are some ways that teens can have a positive influence on their peers.

1. Notice the warning signs—if a friend has become irritable, depressed, or has started falling asleep during class, ask if he or she wants to talk. He or she may tell you to mind your own business, or may start to open up to you about problems. Even if he or she does not take the offer, at least the friend knows that someone cares.

2. Don't go along with a bad plan—if a friend invites you to a pharm party, or wants to hang out and take drugs, do not insult him or her or say negative things about the other attendees or the suggestion. Just say that taking medications that way is very dangerous and you do not want to risk getting sick. Try to offer an alternative activity, like a movie or a trip to the mall. If a youth group is having an activity, invite your friend. Say that it would be better to be in a place where you can talk to each other and not suffer health consequences the next day.

3. Talk to someone who can help—if you feel that the teen is involved too deeply in his or her addiction and you fear for his or her safety, talk to a trusted parent, an older sibling, school counselor, athletic coach, clergyman—anyone who can help.

4. Talk to like-minded friends—other teens who are aware of drug abuse can change the path of addiction. Often, teens turn to a drug-associated peer group because they just want friends. If the teen feels that the non-drug-taking peers will be non-judgmental and friendly, he or she may see that the new group is more fun.

5. Be ready to call for help—if a teen who is on drugs passes out, has a seizure, falls asleep and cannot be awakened, or any other unusual behavior, do not just chalk it up to the drug and wait for the episode to pass. Call 911 for help; let the paramedics know what drug the teen took. Fast action can save another teen's life.

into a drink, this drug causes decreased blood pressure, drowsiness, muscle relaxation, reduced anxiety, dizziness, confusion, and anterograde amnesia, forgetting events that happened after taking the drug. Rohypnol is 10 times more potent than diazepam (Valium). It starts to take effect 15 to 20 minutes after it is taken, and lasts approximately 4 to 12 hours or longer. Flunitrazepam is abused by a wide variety of individuals, including high school students, college students, street gang members, rave party attendees, and heroin and cocaine abusers.[6]

Anterograde amnesia is one of the drug's most hazardous effects. Under the influence of this drug, people have no memory of what happened to them. Because of this, Rohypnol has earned the reputation and nickname "the date rape drug." When somebody takes Rohypnol voluntarily or involuntarily, by having it slipped into a drink, the teen may not be able to remember an assault, who did it, or the events that led up to it. People who slip Rohypnol into a drink can sexually assault their victims with no resistance and sometimes no consequences. Later on, if the victim has been physically hurt or realizes that she or he has been the victim of a rape, there is no memory of the location of the crime and no description of the person who did it. This can result in future physiological and emotional problems for the victim, such as frustration, guilt, and self-blame.

WHEN WORKING TOGETHER IS DEADLY

Synergy is usually a good thing. The word is derived from the Greek *synergos*, meaning working together. With friends, family, or work, synergy has a positive result. A negative type of synergy also results from mixing drugs and alcohol. When drugs and alcohol mix, the total synergistic effect is greater than the independent effects of the two substances.

Alcohol combined with sleep medications such as central nervous system depressants is a very unhealthy and possibly deadly mix. Alcohol produces a synergistic effect when taken with drugs such as sedative-hypnotics, barbiturates, minor tranquilizers, narcotics, codeine, methadone, and some **analgesics**, or pain relievers. Alcohol is a depressant, just like tranquilizers and sleeping pills, which slow bodily functions like breathing and heart rate. When too much alcohol is combined with too many sleeping medications, there is a threat that the body's functions may slow down so much that they completely stop.

SLEEP PATTERNS UP IN SMOKE

While some teens smoke marijuana to relax, a study of its use in adolescents shows that its effect on sleep stages can be serious. Marijuana use is prevalent in the teen population. Nearly half of 12th graders have tried marijuana, and 6% use it daily.[7] Sleep also plays a large role in a teen's daily life. The average teen needs approximately 8.50–9.25 hours of sleep per night. At this age, when sleep phases start to change, teens often do not feel tired enough to fall asleep until later. Marijuana use during adolescence may disrupt sleep structure even more. Chronic marijuana-using adolescents may not only receive less sleep than needed, but the sleep they do receive may be less restorative. Short-term, low-dose marijuana use has been associated with reduced Rapid Eye Movement (REM) sleep (the period associated with vivid dreams) and mild increases in **slow wave sleep (SWS)**, the deepest stage of sleep, characterized by absence of eye movements, decreased body temperature, and involuntary body movements. Stopping marijuana has different but still bad effects on sleep. In a study during two separate 3–5 day periods of abstaining from marijuana, participants reported increased difficulty with sleep initiation and maintenance, as well as "strange dreams." After abstaining, or not taking the drug for about a month, the teens' sleep patterns returned. Teens may recover more rapidly from health issues than adults, possibly leading to a shorter sleep recovery process. Heavy marijuana use also caused periodic limb movements during sleep, which also interrupted sleep. The study noted, "given that 80% of adolescents may be in a state of partial sleep deprivation, the compromised quality of sleep in adolescent marijuana users may render them particularly vulnerable to sleep loss effects." Sleep plays a critical role in a person's transition from childhood to adulthood—biologically, physically, cognitively, psychologically, and socially. Given the consistently high rates of marijuana use among youth, understanding the effects of adolescent marijuana exposure on sleep are important, as this may in turn have long-term effects on brain function, risky behaviors, and mood.

In the body, the liver works to break down and get rid of drugs and alcohol. Alcohol and sleep medications compete for the same types of liver enzymes that break down drugs and flush them from the body. As a result, when alcohol and drugs are in the body at the same time, the liver cannot handle the load and the drug molecules are reabsorbed and recirculated throughout the body. When the sum of these two depressants added together adds up to more than the singular effects, respiratory arrest (stopping breathing) and death can result.[8]

WAKE-UP CALL

In high schools and college campuses across the nation, coffee and caffeinated energy drinks keep many students awake throughout the day. While moderate doses of caffeine, about two to four cups of brewed coffee per day, are not harmful, exceeding the limit can affect the sleep cycle and the body's organs. The Mayo Clinic staff noted that using caffeine to stay awake encourages a sleep deprivation cycle. Caffeinated drinks are consumed to stay awake during the day, but the effects continue so the person is unable to fall asleep at night. After waking up several times during the night (also a side effect of caffeine), the person is extra sleepy in the morning and, once again, may turn to a caffeinated drink to start the day.[9]

When caffeine-containing energy drinks are consumed in large quantities, caffeine toxicity can result, with symptoms such as nervousness, anxiety, restlessness, insomnia, stomach upset, tremors, and fast heart rate.[10] Abuse of caffeine drinks occurs when teens try to counteract sedative drugs or alcohol with energy drinks. The FDA has voiced concerns about the safety of alcoholic beverages with added caffeine because published peer-reviewed studies suggest that drinking beverages containing added caffeine and alcohol is associated with risky behaviors that may lead to hazardous and life-threatening situations. Caffeine can dull some of the senses that an individual might normally rely on to determine how drunk he or she has become. Some energy drinks target their advertising to younger men in particular. An example of this is the drink additive called Blow, which is packaged in glass vials and includes a mirror and what looks like a plastic credit card to imitate cocaine use. Another similar drink additive was even called Cocaine.[11]

While cutting back on caffeine can be difficult and may cause some signs of withdrawal, the symptoms usually go away after a few days.

ADDICTION: A TOUGH PILL TO SWALLOW

Teens do not take drugs expecting to become addicted. Addiction sneaks up on those who start off just wanting to feel good, and then need increased doses to achieve the same effect. Curiosity, peer pressure, or attempts to cover up life's problems are just a few of the reasons that teens try drugs.[12] At first, a drug seems to work to encourage sleep more easily or help someone forget a problem in the medication-induced haze, but then comes the urge to use the drug more frequently and in greater doses.

At first, taking drugs is voluntary, but as the body chemistry changes and the body needs the chemicals more, it becomes very difficult to stop. One of the first obstacles to drug treatment is **denial**, insisting that something is not true despite overwhelming evidence. The teen may underestimate the quantity of drugs being taken, how much of an impact it has on his or her life, and the ability to stop when necessary. When the teen admits there is a problem, drug addiction can be treated.

7
Looking Ahead

Lila had been worried about Marshall for a while before she decided to have a talk with him about how she thought he had been changing lately. They had been friends for a few years, and she knew that Marshall was usually a responsible, funny, helpful guy who she could always count on to help her with her schoolwork or boy problems. Lately, though, Marshall seemed to be distant. When she talked to him, instead of looking her straight in the eye as he had always done before, he seemed disinterested, unfocused. When she asked him what the matter was, he laughed and shrugged, and told her to lighten up; he was just having a bad day. Bad days became bad weeks, and then after a few bad months, Lila wanted her friend back.

Wanting another opinion, she asked another friend, Patrick, if he thought that Marshall was just angry at her. Patrick told her that he had seen Marshall fall asleep during class several times. When he asked what was wrong, Marshall blamed it on his homework that kept him up all hours of the night. While he was usually somewhat competitive with Patrick about grades, he didn't seem to care when the teacher called him in after class to discuss several failing test grades. When Patrick tried to tell Marshall that he could help if he didn't understand some information, Marshall got agitated and changed the subject.

Lila decided to ask a school counselor what to do after Marshall tried to borrow some money. She hadn't seen him in a few days because he had skipped school, and he really didn't seem to be interested in being her friend anymore. But this day, he tried to be friendly, but in a fake sort of way. She saw that he was leading up to something. He asked for some money to pay back a friend. When Lila told him she didn't have any to spare, he told her that he'd see her later, and walked off, looking disappointed and, in Lila's words, "a bit desperate."

Lila feared that Marshall had gotten into a situation that he couldn't handle on his own. She went to a guidance counselor and told him the problem without telling him who her friend was. The counselor said that he would like to get in touch with this person's parents, so that if there was a problem, it could be solved. Lila agreed, although she asked to be anonymous for now. When Marshall's parents came to school, they seemed surprised that the counselor thought that Marshall might have a drug problem. Although they weren't seeing as much of him lately as they used to, he seemed fine most of the time, but somewhat preoccupied, which he blamed on his schoolwork. After hearing about the possible warning signs, his parents grew concerned. They had noticed some small electronic items missing around the house and just thought that they were misplaced. Some money, too, had disappeared from a countertop, but each thought the other had taken it. In a busy house, things like that are easy to miss.

Marshall was asked to attend the next meeting. At first, he was very upset, and accused the counselor and parents of "ambushing" him with all of their questions, which he called accusations. When confronted with the facts of the missing electronics and money, and his recent bad grades, he broke down and started to cry. It was a relief that they found out, he said. He was addicted to sedatives and had been for a few months. It started when he couldn't fall asleep because of some college entrance exams that were coming up. He took some pills that he found in his parents' medicine cabinet. No one noticed that they were gone, and they made him drowsy enough to sleep. They made him feel good, so he continued his new habit. He couldn't take all of them because his parents would notice, so he asked around at school, and got enough to relieve the anxiety that he now also felt during the day. Then he needed more, and then he needed money, and then all that mattered was getting the pills so that he could function at what he thought was a normal level. He stayed away from his friends because he knew that they would guess the truth, and he didn't want to disappoint them or *his parents, but he had no choice and no willpower over his craving for the sedative drugs.*

After a trip to the doctor, Marshall started treatment at a local drug rehabilitation center. He went through withdrawal and had a few setbacks, but now, when he needs to relieve anxiety and fall asleep, he takes some medication prescribed for him by the doctor, and in the right dose. He had to make up some of the classes that he failed, and now, with the support of family and friends, he has the confidence to continue with his college plans.

Researchers and physicians do not take the problem of sleep disorders lying down. They continue to explore the physiology of sleep, correct amounts of sleep, and the types and quality of sleep needed to help people function better while awake. For a teenager, busy schedules, family, school, social life, and work often win in the competition with sleep schedules and cause sleeping disorders. Significant scientific breakthroughs in sleep research have already resulted in many medications that target specific disorders, and others are still being tested for effectiveness and safety.

ON THE DRAWING BOARD AND IN THE LAB

Some medications involve alterations to already existing medications, while others try new avenues to encourage sleep. An article by Dr. David Neubauer, director of the Johns Hopkins Sleep Disorders Center, discussed some of the various breakthroughs that will affect future sleep problems.[1] He noted that scientists are making new compounds in the benzodiazepine receptor agonist (BZRA) category. An agonist is a chemical that binds to the cell's receptor and triggers a response from the cell. Studies into these medications try alternate strategies of delivering the drug to the proper receptors, or try to change the activity of the agonist. One new FDA-approved insomnia drug features a controlled release of the formula. Newer BZRA hypnotics are exploring more effective ways to target the GABA receptors. Some research is geared toward creating hypnotics that bypass stomach absorption to help people fall asleep more rapidly. Besides the way the medication works, scientists also study how the chemicals enter the body so that the drugs can be taken in the middle of the night rather than at bedtime. Clinical trials are being performed with

sublingual, "under the tongue" or orally dissolvable tablets, and inhalation and nasal spray formations. These changes may help to decrease the drugs' effects and avoid next-morning drowsiness.

Clinical trials are also underway on melatonin receptor agonists. The melatonin has a positive effect on disorders related to circadian rhythms, such as delayed sleep phase, as well as conditions related to late work shifts or jet lag. Currently, ramelteon is the only FDA-approved melatonin receptor agonist available in the United States. This type of formula shows promise in helping to start the sleep process. One experimental drug combines melatonin and **serotonin**, a brain chemical that influences depression, in the hopes of improving both insomnia and depression with one pill.

Antihistamines such as diphenhydramine are still popular, but have the drawback of lasting too long. Labs are now testing new drugs that have the same basic ingredients and results but work for a shorter period of time. Some antidepressants have also gained attention for their tendencies to sedate and to increase slow wave sleep. For narcolepsy sufferers, new formulations of amphetamines are being investigated that can be taken at lower doses. While helpful to some, these drugs still have a high potential for abuse.

INFO TO SINK YOUR TEETH INTO

Sleep disorders can also be caused by malocclusion, when the upper and lower teeth do not mesh well, or bruxism, grinding teeth while sleeping. People with these dental conditions may awaken with headaches, a sore jaw, or sore teeth. Dentists who are researching sleep disorders have developed more than 100 FDA-approved oral appliances, each with a different way of managing the sleep breathing disorders.[2]

Investigators of sleep disorders continually search for new, safer medications that will put people to sleep or keep them awake. However, behavioral strategies to change poor sleep patterns should also be practiced. Teens who believe that they are suffering from lack of sleep at night or daytime sleepiness should discuss this problem with a parent, guardian, doctor, or school counselor because insomnia among adolescents is associated with future physical and psychological problems.[3] Clinical psychologist Dr. Michael Breus noted that the brain does not completely finish developing until the early to mid-20s, so a person who has insomnia throughout those critical growth phases for physical and psychological development may be at risk for future health issues.

THE FIRST STEPS

For teens, regulating sleep is complicated. Drugs are easily accessible, misinformation about drug safety abounds, and peer pressure can result in life-threatening misuse of sleep medications. It is up to teens to ask for help in determining the cause of daytime sleepiness or lost sleep, to use prescribed sleep medications responsibly, and to refrain from taking others' medications.

The teenage years are filled with opportunities for learning about oneself and the world. Psychologists who specialize in adolescent development note that three tasks during this time of life are: to develop independence from parents, to discover a potential life career, and to find a compatible life partner. At this vital period for exploration and self-discovery, losing hours to a sleep-drug-induced fog seems like a waste of valuable time. For those who have tried unsuccessfully to treat sleeping disorders on their own, and who have become addicted to any of the many categories of over-the-counter and prescription drugs available on the market, there is help.

As a self-assessment, teens should reflect on the following criteria and see if they have experienced: periods when they do not remember what happened; using drugs when alone because of an uncontrollable urge; losing interest in hobbies, friends, or activities that used to be priorities; poor grades in school or frequent absences; relying on drugs to cope with problems; inability to fall asleep without the drugs; keeping secrets or lying to family and friends; choosing to be alone for an increasing amount of time; stealing or selling possessions to get money to buy drugs; or gradually building a tolerance to get the same effect.

Treatment of drug addiction for teens is different than that for adults, and teens who need substance abuse programs should be referred by their doctor or counselor to a program geared specifically for teens. Successful programs not only help to wean the person off the medication but also work to improve problem-solving and social skills to build self-esteem. Verbal skills are learned, so the teen knows how to ask for help in the future or, more importantly, how to assert the choice to say no. In treatment, the teen should be assessed for other health issues, such as depression, anxiety, and post-traumatic stress disorder, that could cause the sleep disorder. It is important to identify these underlying conditions and find a way to deal with them, too, or else they could flare up again. After treatment, a support system should be in place for any questions, or any time the teen finds that the problem may be resurfacing, or if he or she needs to discuss how to deal with a difficult situation.[4]

SLEEP DRUGS ON TRIAL

People who want to be a part of a controlled process that tests the safety and effectiveness of a sleep drug can take part in a clinical trial. The clinicaltrials.gov Web site, a service of the U.S. National Institutes of Health (NIH), lists the many clinical trials currently underway in the United States. The NIH, through its National Library of Medicine (NLM), developed the site in collaboration with all NIH institutes and the Food and Drug Administration (FDA).The list of trials includes which ones are recruiting, which are active and not recruiting, and which are completed. Some clinical trials are paid, which means that the participants receive a specific fee. Volunteers in paid clinical trials in the United States can receive $100–300 per day.[5] Other trials offer only the medication and medical monitoring during the trial.

Clinicaltrials.gov outlined the benefits and drawbacks to participating in a trial. Well-designed and well-executed clinical trials allow eligible participants to[6]

- play an active role in their own health care.
- gain access to new research treatments before they are widely available.
- obtain expert medical care at leading health care facilities during the trial.
- help others by contributing to medical research.

However, there are risks, including the following:

- There may be unpleasant, serious, or even life-threatening side effects to experimental treatment.

- The experimental treatment may not be effective for the participant.
- The **protocol**, or study plan on which all trials are based, requires time and attention, including trips to the study site, more treatments, hospital stays, or complex dosage requirements.

Trials are sponsored by the NIH, government agencies, the pharmaceutical industry, universities, foundations, and organizations from all over the world.

LIGHTS OUT

It may be difficult to imagine that sleep plays such an important role in a teenager's waking life. Sleep is a time of rejuvenation for the body and mind, not just a waste of several hours every night. While sleep drugs can make problems seem like a dream, disturbing the natural cycles and rhythms of sleep can cause long-term negative results. When taken responsibly, under the direction of a physician, and in conjunction with sleep maintenance measures, sleep medications can help the body stay healthy, refreshed, and fortified enough to tackle the challenges of the new day.

Notes

Chapter 1

1. "Prescription for Danger: A Report on the Troubling Trend of Prescription and Over-the-Counter Drug Abuse Among the Nation's Teens," Office of National Drug Control Policy, January 2008, http://www.ncjrs.gov/App/publications/Abstract.aspx?id=243226 (accessed January 21, 2011).

2. "New Report Shows Teens Moving From Street Drugs to Prescription Drugs," Community Anti-Drug Coalitions of America, http://www.cadca.org/resources/detail/new-report-shows-teens-moving-street-drugs-prescription-drugs (posted March 1, 2007).

3. R. A. Friedman, M.D., "The Changing Face of Teenage Drug Abuse—The Trend Toward Prescription Drugs," *New England Journal of Medicine* 354, 14 (2006): 1448.

4. L. Robinson, G. Kemp, and S. Barston, "Sleeping Pills, Natural Sleep Aids & Medications, What's Best for You?" HelpGuide.org, http://www.helpguide.org/life/sleep_aids_medication_insomnia_treatment.htm (updated September 2010).

5. Sean Esteban McCabe, Carol J. Boyd, James A. Cranford, Christian J. Teter, "Motives for Nonmedical Use of Prescription Opioids Among High School Seniors in the United States—Self-treatment and Beyond," *Archives of Pediatrics and Adolescent Medicine* 163, 8 (2009):739–744, http://archpedi.ama-assn.org/cgi/content/full/163/8/739#BIBL (accessed November 11, 2010).

6. Dennis A. Nutter, Jr., M.D., Guy K. Palmes, M.D., Benyam Tegene, M.D., "Sleep Disorder Problems Associated With Other Disorders" eMedicine from WebMD, http://emedicine.medscape.com/article/916611-overview (updated August 24, 2010).

7. "Circadian Rhythms Fact Sheet," National Institutes of General Medical Sciences, http://www.nigms.nih.gov/

Publications/Factsheet_
CircadianRhythms.htm
(updated September 22, 2010).

8. T. Porkka-Heiskanen, "Adenosine in Sleep and Wakeful-
ness," *Annals of Medicine*
31, 2 (April 1999):125–129,
http://www.ncbi.nlm.nih.gov/
pubmed/10344585 (published
April 1999).

9. "Melatonin and Sleep," National
Sleep Foundation, http://www
.sleepfoundation.org/article/
sleep-topics/melatonin-and-
sleep (accessed November 11,
2010).

10. Mary G. Graham, ed., "Sleep
Needs, Patterns and Difficulties
of Adolescents: Summary of a
Workshop," Forum on Ado-
lescence, Board on Children,
Youth, and Families, National
Research Council, Institute of
Medicine, http://www.nap
.edu/openbook.php?record_
id=9941&page=8 (accessed
November 17, 2010).

11. "Brain Basics: Understanding
Sleep," National Institute of
Neurological Disorders and
Stroke, http://www.ninds.nih
.gov/disorders/brain_basics/
understanding_sleep.htm#
dreaming (updated May 21,
2007).

12. "Coping With Excessive
Sleepiness: Sleep 101," WebMD,
http://www.webmd.com/
sleep-disorders/excessive-
sleepiness-10/sleep-101
(updated January 8, 2010).

13. Craig Lambert, "Deep Into
Sleep," *Harvard Magazine,*
July/August 2005, http://
harvardmagazine.com/2005/07/
deep-into-sleep.html (accessed
November 11, 2010).

14. "2006 Sleep in America Poll,"
National Sleep Foundation,
http://www.sleepfoundation
.org/sites/default/files/2006_
summary_of_findings.pdf
(accessed November 9, 2010).

15. Emily Sohn," Teen Car Crashes
Tied to Early Classes." Discovery News: Kids and Parenting.
MSNBC.com, http://www
.msnbc.msn.com/id/37601601
(updated June 9, 2010).

16. "Sleep Apnea in Children &
Teens Linked to Lower Grades,"
American Academy of Sleep
Medicine, http://www.disabled-
world.com/health/neurology/
sleepdisorders/sleepapnea/
apnea-schooling.php (pub-
lished June 8, 2010).

17. Sarah Spinks, "Inside the Teenage Brain: Adolescents and
Sleep," PBS, http://www
.pbs.org/wgbh/pages/frontline/
shows/teenbrain/from/sleep.
html (accessed November 11,
2010).

18. "Sleep Needs, Patterns and Difficulties of Adolescents: Summary

of a Workshop," Commission on Behavioral and Social Sciences and Education, http://www.nap.edu/catalog.php?record_id=9941#toc (accessed November 11, 2010).

Chapter 2

1. Robert Golden, Fred Peterson, John Haley, *The Truth About Drugs* (New York: Infobase Publishing, 2009).

2. Glen Hanson, Peter Venturelli, Annette Fleckenstein, *Drugs and Society* (Sudbury, Mass.: Jones & Bartlett Publishers, 2006).

3. E. L. Abel, *Marijuana, the First 12,000 Years* (New York: Plenum, 1980).

4. Melissa Stoppler, M.D., "Chloral Hydrate Uses and Risks." MedicineNet.com, http://www.medicinenet.com/script/main/art.asp?articlekey=80075 (posted March 27, 2007).

5. F. Lopez-Munoz, R. Ucha-Udabe, C. Alamo, "The History of Barbituates A Century After Their Clinical Introduction," *Neuropsychiatric Disease and Treatment* 1, 4 (December 2005): 329–343. http://www.ncbi.nlm.nih.gov/pmc/articles/PMC2424120 (accessed November 11, 2010).

6. Eric H.Chudler, "Barbiturates," Neuroscience for Kids, http://faculty.washington.edu/chudler/barb.html (updated October 8, 2010).

7. Richard Ries, Shannon Miller, David Fiellin, Richard Saitz, *Principles of Addiction Medicine* (Philadelphia: Lippincott Williams & Wilkins, 2003).

8. "Benzodiazepines," Center for Substance Abuse Research," http://www.cesar.umd.edu/cesar/drugs/benzos.asp (posted on May 2, 2005).

9. "Side Effects of Sleep Drugs," U.S. Food and Drug Administration, http://www.fda.gov/forconsumers/onsumerupdates/ucm107757.htm (updated October 23, 2010).

10. "Chapter 1—The Controlled Substances Act," U.S. Drug Enforcement Administration, http://www.justice.gov/dea/pubs/abuse/1-csa.htm (accessed November 11, 2010).

Chapter 3

1. "Brain Basics: Understanding Sleep," National Institute of Neurological Disorders and Stroke, http://www.ninds.nih.gov/disorders/brain_basics/understanding_sleep.htm#sleep_disorders (updated May 21, 2007).

2. Mary G. Graham, ed., "Sleep Needs, Patterns and Difficulties of Adolescents: Summary of a Workshop," Forum on Adolescence, Board on

Children, Youth, and Families, National Research Council, Institute of Medicine, http://www.nap.edu/openbook.php?record_id=9941&page=2 (accessed January 19, 2011).

3. "Teens With Insomnia at Increased Risk for Depression, Suicide, Substance Abuse," MedHeadlines, http://medheadlines.com/2008/10/02/teens-with-insomnia-at-increased-risk-for-depression-suicide-substance-abuse (posted October 2008).

4. National Heart and Lung Institute, "What Causes Insomnia?" http://www.nhlbi.nih.gov/health/dci/Diseases/inso/inso_causes.html (accessed February 28, 2011).

5. "An Overview of Insomnia," WebMD, http://www.webmd.com/sleep-disorders/guide/insomnia-symptoms-and-causes (accessed March 3, 2010).

6. Mary G. Graham, ed., "Sleep Needs, Patterns and Difficulties of Adolescents: Summary of a Workshop," Forum on Adolescence, Board on Children, Youth, and Families, National Research Council, Institute of Medicine, http://www.nap.edu/openbook.php?record_id=9941&page=8 (accessed November 12, 2010).

7. "Delayed Sleep Phase Syndrome," Athens Center for Sleep Disorders, http://www.athenssleepcenter.com/PDF/DelayedSleepPhaseSyndrome.pdf (accessed November 4, 2010).

8. "Delayed Sleep Phase Syndrome," Kidzzzsleep. Lifespan Sleep Disorders Center, http://www.kidzzzsleep.org/handouts/delayedsleep.htm (updated September 5, 2009).

9. "Narcolepsy Fact Sheet," National Institute of Neurological Disorders and Stroke, National Institutes of Health, http://www.ninds.nih.gov/disorders/narcolepsy/detail_narcolepsy.htm (updated May 14, 2010).

10. Neil Feldman, M.D., "Narcolepsy: The Differential Diagnosis of Sleepiness and Fatigue," Sleep Disorder Center at Palms of Pasadena Hospital, St. Petersburg, Florida, http://www.dcmsonline.org/jax-medicine/2001journals/March2001/Narcolopsy.htm (accessed November 12, 2010).

11. "Narcolepsy Fact Sheet," National Institute of Neurological Disorders and Stroke, National Institutes of Health, http://www.ninds.nih.gov/disorders/narcolepsy/detail_narcolepsy.htm (updated May 14, 2010).

12. Judy Owens, M.D., and Jodi Minell, *Take Charge of Your Child's Sleep* (New York: Marlowe & Co., 2005), 203.

13. Mayo Clinic Staff, "Narcolepsy Treatment and Drugs," MayoClinic.com, http://www.mayoclinic.com/health/narcolepsy/DS00345/DSECTION=treatments-and-drugs (updated May 15, 2010).

14. "Tired of the Sleepiness?" American Sleep Apnea Association, http://www.sleepapnea.org/resources/brochure.html (accessed November 5, 2010).

15. "Apnea," The Foundation for Better Health Care, http://www.fbhc.org/Patients/Modules/sleepapn.cfm#top (accessed November 4, 2010).

16. "Dreams, Nightmares," PBS Kids, http://pbskids.org/itsmylife/emotions/dreams/article5.html (accessed January 18, 2011).

17. Obringer, Lee Ann, "How Dreams Work," January 27, 2005. HowStuffWorks.com, http://health.howstuffworks.com/mental-health/sleep/dreams/dream.htm (accessed September 29, 2010).

18. "Sleep Apnea," National Heart, Lung and Blood Institute, http://www.nhlbi.nih.gov/health/dci/Diseases/SleepApnea/SleepApnea_Treatments.html (accessed November 4, 2010).

19. "Restless Legs Syndrome in Children and Adolescents," Cleveland Clinic, http://my.clevelandclinic.org/disorders/restless_leg_syndrome/hic_restless_legs_syndrome_in_children_and_adolescents.aspx (accessed November 8, 2010).

20. "Restless Legs Syndrome," Mayo Clinic.com, http://www.mayoclinic.com/health/restless-legs-syndrome/DS00191/DSECTION=treatments-and-drugs (updated December 23, 2009).

21. Mayo Clinic Staff, "Restless Legs Syndrome," MayoClinic.com, http://www.mayoclinic.com/health/restless-legs-syndrome/DS00191/DSECTION=treatments-and-drugs (posted December 3, 2009).

22. "Treatments for Restless Legs Syndrome," WebMD, http://www.webmd.com/sleep-disorders/guide/restless-leg-syndrome-treatment (reviewed March 3, 2010)

Chapter 4

1. "Antihistamines: Understanding Your OTC Options," FamilyDoctor.org, http://familydoctor.org/online/famdocen/home/otc-center/otc-medicines/857.html (updated December 2009).

2. C. H. Ashton, "Benzodiaz-epines, How They Work and How to Withdraw," School of Neurosciences, Division of Psychiatry, The Royal Victoria Infirmary, University of Newcastle, http://www.benzo.org.uk/manual/bzcha01.htm (accessed November 17, 2010).

3. "What are CNS Depressants?," National Institute on Drug Abuse, http://www.nida.nih.gov/researchreports/prescription/prescription3.html (accessed November 15, 2010).

4. "Prescription Depressants," Parents, The Anti-Drug, http://www.theantidrug.com/drug-information/otc-prescription-drug-abuse/prescription-drug-rx-abuse/prescription-depressants.aspx#foot (accessed November 15, 2010).

5. "Insomnia Medications," University of Maryland Medical Center, http://www.umm.edu/patiented/articles/what_drug_treatments_insomnia_000027_8.htm (accessed November 16, 2010).

6. Melinda Beck, "To Cut Risks of Sleeping Pills, Hide Car Keys, Unplug Phone," The Wall Street Journal, http://online.wsj.com/article/SB121001247529168149.html (posted May 6, 2008).

7. "Getting High on Prescription and Over-the-Counter Drugs Is Dangerous: A Guide to Keeping Your Teenager Safe in a Changing World," Partnership for a Drug-Free America, http://www.bnl.gov/hr/occmed/EAP/linkable_files/pdf/TeenPrescriptionDrugAbuse.pdf (accessed November 19, 2010).

8. U.S. Department of Justice, "Methylphenidate A Background Paper," National Criminal Justice Reference Service, (Rockville, Md.: NCJRS Photocopy Services, 1995), Abstract, http://www.ncjrs.gov/App/Publications/abstract.aspx?ID=163349 (accessed November 18, 2010).

9. American Academy of Pain Medicine, "Pain Patients At Risk For Sleep Apnea," Science Daily, http://www.sciencedaily.com/releases/2007/09/070906104140.htm (posted September 11, 2007).

10. "NIDA InfoFacts: Prescription and Over-the-Counter Medications," National Institute On Drug Abuse, http://www.nida.nih.gov/infofacts/painmed.html (updated July 2009).

11. "Insomnia Medications," University of Maryland Medical Center, http://www.umm.edu/patiented/articles/what_drug_treatments_insomnia_000027_8.htm (accessed November 16, 2010).

Chapter 5

1. "Sleep Disorders in the Older Child and Teen," Cleveland Clinic, http://my.clevelandclinic .org/Documents/Sleep_ Disorders_Center/09_ Adolescent_factsheet.pdf (accessed November 24, 2010).
2. "Polysomnography," Medline Plus, National Institutes of Health, http://www.nlm .nih.gov/medlineplus/ency/ article/003932.htm (accessed November 23, 2010).
3. "The Snoozeletter," Neurology & Neuroscience Associates, http://www.nnadoc.com/ snoozeletter_1_10.pdf (accessed November 24, 2010).

Chapter 6

1. Richard A. Friedman, M.D., "The Changing Face of Teenage Drug Abuse—The Trend Toward Prescription Drugs," *New England Journal of Medicine* 354, 14 (2006): 1448, http://www.ca-cpi.org/ Research_Corner/1448.pdf (accessed April 17, 2007).
2. "Results from the 2009 National Survey on Drug Use and Health: Volume I. Summary of National Findings," U.S. Department of Health and Human Services, Substance Abuse and Mental Health Ser- vices Administration, Office of Applied Studies, NSDUH Series H-38A, HHS Publication No. SMA 10–4586 Findings, http:// www.oas.samhsa.gov/ NSDUH/2k9NSDUH/ 2k9ResultsP.pdf (posted September 2010).
3. "Prescription Drug Abuse," NIDA (National Institute on Drug Abuse) for Teens, http://teens.drugabuse.gov/ facts/facts_rx1.php (accessed November 24, 2010).
4. "Prescription Drug Abuse Chart," National Institute on Drug Abuse, http://www .nida.nih.gov/DrugPages/ PrescripDrugsChart.html (accessed November 27, 2010).
5. "Know the Trends: Rave Parties," Parents, The Anti-Drug, http:// www.theantidrug.com/ei/ trends_raves.asp (accessed November 27, 2010).
6. Terrance Woodworth, "DEA Congressional Testimony," House Commerce Committee Subcommittee on Oversight and Investigations, Drug Enforcement Administration, United States Department of Justice, March 11, 1999, http://www.justice.gov/dea/ pubs/cngrtest/ct990311.htm (accessed November 27, 2010).
7. J. Jacobus, S. Bava, M. Cohen-Zion, O. Mahmood, and S. F. Tapert, "Functional Con- sequences of Marijuana Use in

Adolescents," *Pharmacology Biochemistry and Behavior*; 92, 4 (2009 June): 559–565, http://www.ncbi.nlm.nih.gov/pmc/articles/PMC2697065 (posted April 5, 2009).

8. Christina Dye, "Drugs & Alcohol: Simple Facts About Alcohol-Drug Combinations," Do It Now Foundation, http://www.doitnow.org/pages/121.html (posted March 2010).

9. Mayo Clinic Staff, "Caffeine: How Much is Too Much?" MayoClinic.com, http://www.mayoclinic.com/health/caffeine/NU00600 (posted March 24, 2009).

10. C. J. Reissig, et al., "Caffeinated Energy Drinks: A Growing Problem," Drug Alcohol Depend (2008), http://www.ncbi.nlm.nih.gov/pubmed/18809264 (accessed January 13, 2011).

11. Eugene McCormick, "First There Was Cocaine, Now There is Blow Energy Drink," *Cleveland Leader*, http://www.clevelandleader.com/node/4679 (published February 09, 2008).

12. Melinda Smith, and Joanna Saisan, contributors, "Drug Abuse and Addiction: Signs, Symptoms, and Help for Drug Problems and Substance," Helpguide.org, http://helpguide.org/mental/drug_substance_abuse_addiction_signs_effects_treatment.htm (updated November 2010).

Chapter 7

1. David Neubauer, M.D., "New Directions in the Pharmacologic Treatment of Sleep Disorders," *Primary Psychiatry* 16 (2009): 52–58, http://mbldownloads.com/0209PP_Neubauer.pdf (accessed November 28, 2010).

2. "Sleep Disorders Dentistry," Academy of Clinical Sleep Disorders Dentistry, http://www.acsdd.org/sleep-disorders-dentistry (accessed November 29, 2010).

3. Michael Breus, "Sleep Well," WebMD.com, http://blogs.webmd.com/sleep-disorders/2009/04/teens-and-troubled-sleep.html (posted April 8, 2009).

4. "Treating Teens for Substance Abuse," Drug Rehab Treatment Centers, http://www.drugrehabtreatment.com (accessed November 29, 2010).

5. "What Are Paid Clinical Trials?" Trialscentral.org, http://www.trialscentral.org/paid-clinical-trials.html (accessed November 30, 2010).

6. "Understanding Clinical Trials," Clinicaltrials.gov, http://clinicaltrials.gov/ct2/info/understand#Q02 (updated September 20, 2007).

Glossary

accelerometer   a type of meter that records movement

actigraph   a small, wristwatch-like device applied at a sleep center that is worn for seven days to assess sleep patterns over time

acute insomnia   when sleeplessness lasts only for a short time

adenosine   a chemical messenger that sends signals to the body that it is time for sleep

agonist   a chemical that binds to the cell's receptor and triggers a response from the cell

allergen   a substance that is capable of producing an allergic reaction

alpha-2 agonists   drugs that stimulate alpha-2 receptors in the brain stem, activating nerve cells that quiet the part of the nervous system that controls muscle movements and sensations

analgesic   medicine used to relieve pain

anaphylaxis   a full-body allergic reaction to a drug

angioedema   hive-like swelling

antihistamine   a drug used to counteract the effects of histamine

anxiolytic   anxiety-reducing medication

apnea   a sleep disorder in which a person stops breathing for short periods throughout the night

attention-deficit/ hyperactivity disorder   a condition that makes it difficult to concentrate or sit still

benzodiazepines   a group of drugs used to decrease emotional stress, lessen anxiety, and bring about sleep

biological clock   one of the body's internal mechanisms that controls how often various functions or activities occur, such as sleep cycles

blood-brain barrier   the protective network of blood vessels and cells that filters blood flowing to the brain

chronic insomnia   when sleeplessness lasts for a long time, at least three nights a week for a month or longer

circadian rhythm   in humans and most other animals, an internal clock that is synchronized with light-dark cycles and other cues in the environment

codeine   a drug derived from opium

cortex   area of the brain that controls awareness, thought, and language

cortisol   a hormone released in response to stress

delayed sleep phase syndrome   a sleep disorder characterized by delaying falling asleep for two or more hours

denial   insisting that something is not true despite overwhelming evidence

desaturations   abnormal drops in the oxygen rate

dopamine   a chemical messenger in the brain

dyssomnias   disorders that cause difficulty in starting or maintaining sleep

epilepsy   a central nervous system disorder characterized by loss of consciousness and seizures

Epworth Sleepiness Scale   an eight-question assessment for determining whether a sleep disorder is present

gamma-aminobutyric acid   a natural brain chemical that decreases brain activity and causes calmness

glucose tolerance   the ability of muscle cells and the liver to remove glucose from the bloodstream

hallucinations   seeing, hearing, or smelling things that are not there

hippocampus   memory area of the brain

histamines   chemicals released by the immune system in allergic reactions

hypoapnea   when breathing is partially blocked for 10 seconds

immune system   a complex system that protects the body against infections and foreign substances

insomnia   continuing sleeplessness

insulin resistance   the body's inability to respond to and use the insulin it produces; can result in obesity and high blood pressure

leptin   substance secreted by fat cells that acts in the brain to inhibit appetite

lucid dreaming   when the sleeper is aware that he or she is dreaming and is able to participate in the dream's events and change the outcome

melatonin   a hormone secreted by the pineal gland

microsleeps   short naps that last a few seconds, that happen as a result of sleep deprivation

morphine   a powerful, habit-forming narcotic created from opium

narcolepsy   a sleep disorder characterized by suddenly falling asleep during the daytime

neurotransmitter   an agent that transmits messages from one brain cell to another

night terrors   a sleep disorder that may include anxiety, extreme panic, screaming, fast breathing, and sweating

non-Rapid Eye Movement sleep   the first four stages of the sleep cycle

opiate   originating from opium

opioids   drugs that originate from the poppy flower and its product opium

opium   a bitter, brownish addictive narcotic drug that consists of the dried latex obtained from immature seed capsules of the opium poppy

paralysis   loss of the ability to move a body part

parasomnias   disorders that cause disruption of existing sleep

Parkinson's disease   a disorder of the central nervous system characterized by shaking and impaired muscle coordination

periodic limb movement disorder   a sleep disorder that is characterized by rhythmic leg movements during sleep

pineal gland   a small gland located deep within in the brain that secretes melatonin and helps the body to regulate sleep

polysomnogram   a diagnostic sleep study

primary insomnia   lack of sleep caused by conditions unrelated to health, such as stress, travel, or work

protocol   A study plan on which all clinical trials are based. A protocol describes what types of people may participate in the trial; the schedule of tests, procedures, medications, and dosages; and the length of the study. The research staff meets with participants to monitor their health and to determine the safety and effectiveness of their treatment.

pulse oximetry   a sleep test using selected wavelengths of light to determine the oxygen saturation in the blood

raves   high energy, all-night dance parties and clubs that feature dance music with a fast, pounding beat and choreographed laser programs

rebound   when symptoms return more severely than before taking the drug

rebound insomnia   a condition that makes it even harder for the person to fall asleep after medication wears off

REM Sleep   Rapid Eye Movement, the fifth stage of the sleep cycle, characterized by irregular breathing and heart rate and some muscle paralysis

restless legs syndrome   a sleep disorder characterized by the irresistible urge to move the legs

secondary insomnia   lack of sleep caused by a health condition, such as pain, heartburn, or asthma

sedative-hypnotic   a drug that reduces anxiety and causes sleep

selective serotonin or norepinephrine reuptake inhibitors   a class of antidepressant drugs

serotonin   a brain chemical that influences depression

sleep debt   when the effects of lost sleep accumulate

sleep phase delay   the tendency to fall asleep later and wake up later

slow wave sleep   the deepest stage of sleep, characterized by absence of eye movements, decreased body temperature, and involuntary body movements

spongia somnifera   sponges soaked in wine and herbs to promote sleep; used during the Middle Ages

sublingual   under the tongue

suprachiasmatic nucleus   a group of nerve cells in the brain that control the circadian rhythms

sympathetic nervous system   involved in fight-or-flight responses, blood pressure, heartbeat, and digestion

synergy   the condition produced when drugs and alcohol or two drugs are mixed together whereby the result is greater than the independent effects of the two substances

tolerance   a medical phenomenon by which the body becomes increasingly resistant to a drug as a result of exposure to that same drug

further Resources

Books

Karen Bellenir. *Sleep Information for Teens*. Holmes, Pa.: Omnigraphics, Inc., 2007.

Faith Hickman Brynie. *101 Questions About Sleep And Dreams: That Kept You Awake Nights...Until Now*. Breckenridge, Colo.: Twenty-First Century Books, 2006.

Joan Esherick. *Drug Therapy and Sleep Disorders*. Broomall, Pa.: Mason Crest Publishers, 2007.

Robert Golden, Fred Peterson, and John Haley. *The Truth About Drugs*. New York: Infobase Publishing, 2009.

Sandra Augustyn Lawton, editor. *Drug Information for Teens*. Holmes, Pa.: Omnigraphics, 2006.

Andrea Petersen. "Grown-Up Problems Start at Bedtime." *The Wall Street Journal*. January 18, 2011.

Judy Monroe Peterson. *Frequently Asked Questions about Sleep and Sleep Deprivation*. New York: Rosen Publishing Group, Inc., 2010.

Charles P. Pollak, Michael J. Thorpy, and Jan Yager. *The Encyclopedia of Sleep and Sleep Disorders* . New York: Facts On File, 2009.

Web Sites

American Academy of Sleep Medicine
http://www.aasmnet.org

HealthCommunities.com
http://www.sleepdisorderchannel.com/

Healthtree
http://www.healthtree.com/articles/sleep-disorders

National Association of School Psychologists
http://www.nasponline.org/resources/health_wellness/sleep
   disorders_ho.aspx

National Center on Sleep Disorders Research
National Heart, Lung, and Blood Institute, NIH
http://www.nhlbi.nih.gov/about/ncsdr/index.htm

National Institute on Neurological Disorders and Stroke
http://www.ninds.nih.gov/

National Sleep Foundation
http://www.sleepfoundation.org

NIDA (National Institute on Drug Abuse) for Teens
http://teens.drugabuse.gov/

Teen's Health from Nemours
http://kidshealth.org/teen/

Index

About the Author

Mali Rebecca Schantz-Feld is a professional writer and researcher with 20 years of experience. She has won awards for writing from the Florida Magazine Association, the Florida Freelance Writers Association, and the American Business Media. She is a member of the American Medical Writers Association, Florida Magazine Association, Society of American Business Editors and Writers, and the Florida Freelance Writers Association/Cassell Network of Writers.

About the Consulting Editor

Consulting editor **David J. Triggle, Ph.D.,** is a SUNY Distinguished Professor and the University Professor at the State University of New York at Buffalo. These are the two highest academic ranks of the university. Professor Triggle received his education in the United Kingdom with a Ph.D. degree in chemistry from the University of Hull. Following postdoctoral fellowships at the University of Ottawa (Canada) and the University of London (United Kingdom) he assumed a position in the School of Pharmacy at the University at Buffalo. He served as chairman of the Department of Biochemical Pharmacology from 1971 to 1985 and as Dean of the School of Pharmacy from 1985 to 1995. From 1996 to 2001 he served as Dean of the Graduate School and from 1999 to 2001 was also the University Provost. He is currently the University Professor, in which capacity he teaches bioethics and science policy, and is President of the Center for Inquiry Institute, a think tank located in Amherst, New York, and devoted to issues around the public understanding of science. In the latter respect he is a major contributor to the online M.Ed. program—"Science and The Public"—in the Graduate School of Education and The Center for Inquiry.